Revolti
For Ten Year Olds

Helen Paiba is known as one of the most committed, knowledgeable and acclaimed children's booksellers in Britain. For more than twenty years she owned and ran the Children's Bookshop in Muswell Hill, London, which under her guidance gained a superb reputation for its range of children's books and for the advice available to its customers.

Helen was involved with the Booksellers Association for many years and served on both its Children's Bookselling Group and the Trade Practices Committee. In 1995 she was given honorary life membership of the Booksellers Association of Great Britain and Ireland in recognition of her outstanding services to the association and to the book trade. In the same year the Children's Book Circle (sponsored by Books for Children) honoured her with the Eleanor Farjeon Award, given for distinguished service to the world of children's books.

She retired in 1995 and now lives in London.

Titles available in this series

Funny Stories for Five Year Olds
Magical Stories for Five Year Olds
Animal Stories for Five Year Olds
Adventure Stories for Five Year Olds
Bedtime Stories for Five Year Olds

Funny Stories for Six Year Olds
Magical Stories for Six Year Olds
Animal Stories for Six Year Olds
Adventure Stories for Six Year Olds
Bedtime Stories for Six Year Olds

Funny Stories for Seven Year Olds
Scary Stories for Seven Year Olds
Animal Stories for Seven Year Olds
Adventure Stories for Seven Year Olds

Funny Stories for Eight Year Olds
Scary Stories for Eight Year Olds
Animal Stories for Eight Year Olds
Adventure Stories for Eight Year Olds

Funny Stories for Nine Year Olds
Scary Stories for Nine Year Olds
Animal Stories for Nine Year Olds
Adventure Stories for Nine Years Olds
Revolting Stories for Nine Year Olds

Funny Stories for Ten Year Olds
Scary Stories for Ten Year Olds
Animal Stories for Ten Year Olds
Adventure Stories for Ten Year Olds
Revolting Stories for Ten Year Olds

Coming soon
School Stories for Seven Year Olds
School Stories for Eight Year Olds

Revolting

STORIES

For Ten Year Olds

COMPILED BY HELEN PAIBA

ILLUSTRATED BY JUDY BROWN

MACMILLAN
CHILDREN'S BOOKS

First published 2001 by Macmillan Children's Books
a division of Macmillan Publishers Limited
25 Eccleston Place, London SW1W 9NF
Basingstoke and Oxford
www.macmillan.com

Associated companies throughout the world

ISBN 0 330 48372 2

1 3 5 7 9 8 6 4 2

A CIP catalogue record for this book is available from the
British Library.

Typeset by SX Composing DTP, Rayleigh, Essex
Printed and bound in Great Britain by
Mackays of Chatham plc, Kent

Contents

What's for Dinner?

Robert Swindells

"It's Friday," Sammy Troy complained. "Fish and chip day. Why are we having shepherd's pie?"

"I don't know, do I?" said Jane. They were twins but Sammy was ten minutes younger and ten years dafter. Jane spent half her time at school keeping him out of trouble. She swallowed a forkful of the pie. "It's very tasty anyway. Try it."

Sammy tried it. It was good, but he wasn't going to admit it. He'd been looking forward to fish and chips and shepherd's pie just wasn't the same. He pulled a face.

"Pigfood."

"Don't be silly," said Jane, but she knew he would be. He usually was.

Sammy left most of his dinner, and in the playground afterwards he made up a rap. It was about the school cook, and it went like this:

1

"Elsie Brook is a useless cook
If you eat school dinners it's your hard luck
They either kill or make you ill
If the meat don't do it then the custard will."

It wasn't true. Mrs Brook did good dinners, but the rap caught on and a long snake of chanting children wound its way about the playground with Sammy at its head. Jane didn't join in. She thought it was stupid and hoped Mrs Brook wouldn't hear it.

On Saturday, Sammy practised the rap with some of his friends. They meant to get it going again at break on Monday, but at the end of morning assembly the Head said, "I'm sorry to have to tell you all that our Mrs Brook was taken ill over the weekend and will not be here to cook for us this week."

Some of the boys grinned and nudged one another. Sammy whispered in Jane's ear, "She must've eaten some of that shepherd's pie." Jane jabbed him with her elbow.

"However," continued the Head, "we are very lucky to have with us Mr Hannay, who will see to our meals till Mrs Brook returns. Mr Hannay is not only a first-class chef but an explorer as well. He has travelled as cook on a number of expeditions to remote regions, and is famous for his ability to produce appetizing meals from the most unpromising ingredients."

"He'll feel at home here, then," muttered Sammy. "We have the most unpromising ingredients in Europe."

A chef, though! A first-class chef. Morning lessons seemed to drag on for ever. It felt like three o'clock when the buzzer went, though it was five to twelve as always. Hands were washed in two seconds flat, and everybody hurried along to the dining area which was filled with a delicious mouth-watering aroma. Snowy cloths covered all the tables, and on each table stood a little pot of flowers. "Wow!" breathed Jeanette Frazer. "It's like a posh restaurant."

And the food. Oh, the food. First came a thick, fragrant soup which was green but tasted absolutely fantastic. To follow the soup there was a beautiful main course – succulent nuggets of tender white meat in a golden, spicy sauce with baby peas and crispy roast potatoes. And for pudding there were giant helpings of chocolate ice cream with crunchy bits in it.

Sammy licked the last smear of ice cream from his spoon, dropped the spoon in his dish, pushed the dish away and belched. Some of the boys giggled, but his sister glared at him across the table. Sammy smiled. "Sorry, but what a meal, eh? What a stupendous

pig-out. I'll probably nod off in biology this aft."

He didn't though. Miss Corbishley didn't give him the chance. The class was doing pond life, and when they walked in the room the teacher said, "Jane and Sammy Troy, take the net and specimen jar, go down to the pond and bring back some pond beetles and a water boatman or two. Quickly now."

The school pond lay in a hollow beyond the playing field. Rushes grew thickly round its marshy rim and there were tadpoles, newts and dragonflies as well as sticklebacks and the beetles they'd study today. It was Sammy's favourite spot, but today all the creatures seemed to be hiding. No dragonflies

4

darted away as the twins waded through the reeds. No sticklebacks scattered like silver pins when Jane trawled the net through the pondweed, and when she lifted it out it was empty.

"Try again," said Sammy. "Faster."

Jane sent the net swooping through the underwater forest, but all she got was a plume of weed.

"Everything seems to have gone," she said. "And Miss is waiting."

"I know," said Sammy. "She'll think we've wagged off school."

"Don't be ridiculous!" cried Miss Corbishley, when Jane told her there was nothing in the pond. "Only this morning Mr Hannay was saying what a well-stocked pond we have at Milton Middle." The twins were sent to their seats in disgrace, while Jeannette Frazer and Mary Bain went to try their luck. Miss Corbishley made a giant drawing of a water boatman on the board and the children began copying it into their books.

"Hey, Jane!" hissed Sammy. His sister looked at him. He had a funny look on his face. "I've just had a thought."

"Congratulations," she whispered. "I knew you would some day."

"No, listen. You know what Miss said, about Mr Hannay?"

"What about it?"

"He said the pond was well-stocked, right? And now it isn't. And we had that fantastic dinner, only we didn't really know what it was?"

"What's dinner got to do with—?" Jane broke off and gazed at her brother. She shook her head. "No, Sammy. No. That's sick. It's impossible."

"Is it?" Sammy jabbed a finger at her. "What was that soup, then? Green soup. And the meat. And those crunchy bits in the ice cream – what were they?"

Before Jane could reply, Jeanette and Mary came back with long faces and an empty jar.

Walking home that afternoon Jane said, "It's a coincidence, that's all. It can't be true what you're thinking, Sammy." She wasn't sure though, and Sammy certainly wasn't convinced. "I wonder what we'll get tomorrow?" he said.

Tuesday's dinner turned out to be every bit as delicious as Monday's. The twins had kept their suspicions to themselves, so there were no spoilt appetites as the children settled down to eat. Even Jane and Sammy felt better. After all, even Mr Hannay couldn't conjure food from an empty pond.

The soup was orange and there were no lumps in it.

It had plenty of flavour though, and everybody enjoyed it. The main course was Italian – mounds of steaming pasta and a rich, meaty tomato sauce. "If this is how they eat in Italy," said Sammy, "I'm off to live there." He seemed to have forgotten about yesterday. Jane hadn't, but she knew macaroni when she saw it, and this was definitely macaroni.

Tuesday afternoon was C.D.T. with Mr Parker. When the kids arrived he was kneeling in front of his big cupboard, surrounded by a mountain of dusty old drawings, and broken models made from balsa wood and cardboard boxes. "Lost something, sir?" asked Sammy.

Mr Parker nodded. "I'm afraid I have, lad. I could've sworn they were in here."

"What, sir?"

"Some pictures I did with a first-year class three, maybe four years ago. Collage pictures."

"What are they, sir?"

"Oh, you know – you stick things on a sheet of paper to make a picture. Seashells, lentils, bits of macaroni. Any old rubbish you can find, really."

Sammy gulped. "Bits of macaroni, sir?"

"That's right."

"Four years ago, sir?"

"Yes. I'm sure I saw them at the back of the cupboard quite recently and made a mental note to clear them out before the mice got to them."

"Are there mice in your cupboard, sir?" There was a greenish tint to Sammy's face.

"Oh yes, lad. Mice, moths, woodlice, cockroaches. The odd rat, probably. It's a miniature zoo, this cupboard."

Sammy didn't enjoy C.D.T. that afternoon. He couldn't concentrate. He kept picturing old Hannay in his blue and white striped apron, rooting through Parker's cupboard. When he glanced across at Jane he thought she looked unwell. He wondered how Mrs Brook was getting along, and when the boys did the rap at break he didn't join in.

On Wednesday, Jane and Sammy decided they wouldn't eat school lunch unless they knew what it was. Sammy said, "How do we find out what it is?"

"We ask," Jane told him. At eleven o'clock she stuck her hand up and asked to go to the toilet but went to the kitchen instead. Mr Hannay wasn't there, but Mrs Trafford was. "Where's Mr Hannay?" asked Jane. She hoped he'd left, but Mrs Trafford said, "He's just slipped along to the gym, dear. Why – who wants him?"

"Oh, nobody," said Jane. "I was wondering what's for dinner, that's all."

"Opek," said Mrs Trafford.

"Pardon?" said Jane.

"Opek. It's a very old oriental dish, Mr Hannay says. Very nice."

Opek turned out to be a grey, porridge mush. It didn't look all that promising, but it was probably what ancient oriental grub was supposed to look like and it tasted fine. Everybody was enjoying it till Gaz Walker fished a small flat rectangular object from his plate and held it up.

"Here," he complained. "Why is there a Size 4 tag in my dinner?"

"Let's have a look." Jane took the tag and examined it. It looked like the sort of tag you'd find inside a shoe. "Opek," she murmured, wondering why Mr Hannay had been in the gym when he was supposed to be cooking. "Opek." An idea formed in her head and sank slowly into her stomach where it lay like a lead weight. She put the tag on the rim of her plate and sat back with her hands across her stomach. All round the table, kids stopped eating and watched her.

"What's up, Jane?" Sammy's voice was husky.

"Opek," whispered Jane. "I think I know what it means."

"What does it mean?" asked Jeanette, who had almost cleared her plate.

9

"I think it's initials," said Jane. "Standing for Old P.E. Kit."

The peace of the dining area was shattered by cries of revulsion and the scrape and clatter of chairs as everybody on Jane's table stampeded for the door. The kids at the other tables watched till they'd gone, then lowered their heads and went on eating opek.

Sometimes two people can keep a secret, but never ten. There were ten kids at Jane and Sammy's table, and so the secret came out. Nobody went in to dinner on Thursday. Nobody. At twelve o'clock Mr Hannay raised the hatch and found himself gazing at twelve empty tables. He frowned at his watch. Shook it. Raised it to his ear. At five-past twelve he took off his apron and went to see the Head. They stood at the Head's window, looking towards the playing field. All the children were there, and some seemed to be eating the grass. "Good lord," sighed the Head. "What did you cook, Hannay?"

"Epsatsc," said the chef.

"Never heard of it," said the Head. "What is it?"

"Traditional Greek dish," said Hannay smoothly, easily fooling the Head. Jane, who'd got the word from Mrs Trafford, wasn't fooled. "Epsatsc," she said, grimly, leaning on a goalpost. "Erasers, pencil shavings and the school cat."

On Friday everybody brought sandwiches but they

needn't have, because Hannay had gone and Mrs Brook was back. When they spotted her crossing the playground at five to nine the kids cheered. Mrs Brook, who was the sentimental type, had to wipe her eyes before she could see to hang up her coat. The kids chucked their butties in the bin and Sammy's rap was dead.

Dinner wasn't fish and chips, but there were no complaints. Everybody tucked in with gusto – even Sammy. The snowy cloths had gone and there were no flowers, but there was something else instead. Contentment. You could feel it all around.

And so the school week drew to a close. Everybody relaxed. The work was done. The weekend, bright with promise, lay ahead. At half-past three the kids spilled whooping into the yard and away down the drive. Jane and Sammy, in no rush, strolled behind. At the top of the drive stood the gardener, looking lost. Sammy grinned. "What's up, Mr Tench?" The gardener lifted his cap and scratched his head. "Nay," he growled. "There were a pile of nice, fresh horse manure here this morning and it's gone."

The twins exchanged glances. Mrs Brook was coming down the drive. They ran to her. "Mrs Brook!" cried Sammy. "That Mr Hannay – he has left, hasn't he?"

The cook nodded. "Yes, dear, I'm afraid he has but

don't worry – he left me his recipe book, and you know it's just amazing the meals you can get out of stuff you find lying around."

The Changing

Rob Marsh

Saturday

We left home this morning at six and everyone was in a good mood, even Mark's dad whose job it was to take us all the way from the township to the forest station, which was our starting off point. He'd promised to pick us up on Monday afternoon at the other end of the trail. Sean, who's done this particular hike once before, said the first day was the worst. Also we'd have to walk a good 19 kilometres in order to get to the first hut, a lot of it being uphill. I felt my enthusiasm for this trip suddenly beginning to vanish! "The sooner we start, the sooner we finish," Sean added brightly. Mark and I groaned in response. We'd never walked that far before. I pulled a face at Sean and made a joke about collapsing with exhaustion and having to be air-lifted out by the 911 people, like they do on television. Sean puffed noisily as he put his

13

bulging back-pack on and then started to stagger along the path like a drunk. Mark and I copied him, pretending to grunt and groan with the effort. If anyone was watching, the three of us must have looked like we'd just escaped from the mad-house! Luckily, there were only a few birds about and the odd squirrel or two, so I don't suppose they would tell.

Sean had a map of the area and he had marked out the route we were going to follow with a red pen. At first the line zig-zagged through an area labelled "forest", then moved out of the trees to the first hut, where the contours were very close together. Because mapwork was about the only part of geography I bothered listening to, I knew that contours joined land of equal height and that the closer they were together, the steeper the slope. I could see we had some hard climbing ahead of us.

On the second day, we stayed high up in the mountains and then dropped sharply into a river valley where the second hut was situated. Sean said that the third day would be easy. In the morning we'd follow the river for quite a long way and then have a short, steep climb up to the road where Mark's dad would be waiting for us. To start with, the track was wide and fairly flat and we were all in good spirits, chatting all the time but after an hour or so the land started to rise and the going got tougher. Everyone became less chatty after that. We didn't slow down, though, at least not at first. Later on, the track became very steep and the trees started to thin out, and then the forest ended. It was as if we'd reached an invisible border or something. Of course, the track just kept on going, zig-zagging higher and higher until it vanished into the distance.

It was about eleven o'clock by then and we'd been walking for almost four hours. Sean suggested we take out the padkos and rest in the shade while we still had the chance. Mark and I didn't say anything. We just looked at each other, dropped our backpacks, and then slumped down on the ground. I was hot and sweaty by this time and I could see Mark was also out of breath, so it wasn't as if we needed any further encouragement! We fell in a heap.

The place we'd stopped for a rest seemed to be overrun with spiderwebs, especially in the undergrowth. I didn't take much notice of them. Believe me, I won't make that mistake again!

Sean and Mark sat back-to-back on a tree-stump and I made myself comfortable against a fallen tree that was lying next to the track. After I'd taken a long swig from my water-bottle I rolled up my shirt-sleeves and then leaned back with my eyes closed and my arms behind my head. It was a warm day and I was feeling pleasantly tired. I remember also that there were some birds twittering in the trees nearby. I started to doze off . . .

That's when I felt the terrible pain in my arm.

I'd been stung! I jumped up, just in time to see a big, black, hairy thing with long spindly legs dart out of view beneath the log.

"Ag! No! I've been bitten by a spider," I shouted. My shouts alerted my two friends.

By the time the other two came over to me there was a small red swelling on my arm, just below my elbow and it felt like someone was pushing a red-hot needle into the flesh. My whole arm hurt and I kept

rubbing the spot where I'd been bitten as hard as I could, but it didn't seem to make any difference. The pain kept running up and down my arm in hot pulses.

Sean immediately went down on his knees, looking around at the other side of the log. "What sort of spider was it?" he asked.

I thought that was a silly question. How would I know what sort of spider it was? Anyway, my arm was sore.

"I don't know. It didn't leave a name and number," I said sarcastically. That made Sean look up at me. "Oh," he said, but Mark just started to giggle. "And I don't suppose you managed to get a forwarding address either?" he asked.

That's when we all saw the funny side, and we all began laughing and fooling about, making spider jokes and doing spider impressions. Before we set off again, Sean put some antiseptic cream on my arm and the pain started to go away, except for the place where the spider had bitten me, which was still very sore.

I forgot about the spider-bite for a while after that and it wasn't until three hours later that I began to feel strange.

It's hard to describe what it was like. I felt stiff all over for one thing, but it was not muscle stiffness. This stiffness was in the bones. I found it difficult to

17

bend at the waist. I felt like a machine which needed oiling. I tingled all over and my eyes started doing strange things as well. Sometimes everything in the distance became woozy. Then at other times everything split up, as if I was looking out of a window where the glass had cracked into a hundred pieces. I kept blinking to get my sight back but it didn't seem to help at all and it made me feel very dizzy.

I think Sean noticed something was wrong because at one point I caught him glancing over at me with a worried look on his face.

"You all right, Jo?" he asked. I put on a brave face and said yes, everything was fine. Actually I thought I'd had a bit too much sun but I didn't want to say anything in case the others thought I was a sissy. Then my arm started to ache again and I knew the way I was feeling had something to do with the spider-bite. That frightened me because I knew that some spiders are poisonous. I think I would've said something, but Mark, who was walking quite a way ahead of Sean and myself at the time, suddenly shouted that he'd spotted the hut. That made me feel a lot better because I thought I'd be all right if I could just rest for a while.

The hut had been built in a natural hollow just below the summit of the hill we were on. It looked like a big garden shed with a door at one end and a stone fireplace at the other. It had four windows, two on either side and six double bunks. Outside, was a drop toilet the size of a telephone box, a stone braai area (though there wasn't a bit of wood in sight) and a long stainless-steel sink with a tap next to a big concrete water-tank.

At first, we sat around trying to get our breath back or, as Mark put it "chewing the breeze". Then Sean got down to the job of making food. He said he was so hungry he could eat a horse and couldn't wait any longer.

We'd taken food provisions which would be easy to cook. The easier the better was our motto. Sean was opening a can of baked beans. The smell of cooking drifted over to me but I wasn't hungry. I just wanted to find a dark corner and sleep. But when I closed my eyes my head started to spin and there were bright flashes, like fireworks, going off in my head. Also, my arm was beginning to trouble me again and I couldn't stop scratching it. It didn't seem to be swelling or anything. All I could see were two tiny red puncture marks, or small pinpricks on the skin.

I didn't eat a thing that night but Mark and Sean had two plates of baked beans each, as well as a Bar One and a packet of crisps for dessert.

"Why are you not eating?" Mark asked. I just

shrugged and said I wasn't hungry.

"But you keep scratching your arm. Is that bite still hurting?"

"I'm just feeling a bit weird, that's all," I explained and then pulled my sleeve back to prove to them that there was nothing wrong.

Where the spider had bitten me, the skin was bright red. The swelling was as big as an egg.

Sean's eyes opened really wide. "Wow, that looks really bad," he said.

"Ja, like it's poisoned or something . . ."

I suddenly felt all hot and scared.

"It wasn't there a minute ago," I started to explain, then I went quiet because I didn't want to talk about it. Sean was fishing in his bag for the antiseptic again, but I knew that wouldn't do any good.

"It'll go down soon," I said.

"Ja, it's just a scratch that's been infected," Mark said but I could see from his face that he was worried. But the funny thing was, it did go down, just like I'd said it would. An hour later my arm looked as normal as ever, and I felt much better. When I showed the others my arm I could see they were relieved it wasn't getting any worse. And so was I for that matter. The last thing I wanted was to come down with blood poisoning or some other dreaded fever!

I think we all felt quite relieved when we finally

switched off the torches and climbed into our sleeping-bags that night.

Sunday

I woke up with a jolt. It was about three o'clock in the morning. I'd had a strange dream. It was after dark and I'd been in the street outside my house. On either side of the road was a line of big old trees and somehow I'd made a web out of thin shimmery stuff and positioned it from the trunk of one of the trees across the pavement to somebody's front wall.

The whole street was bathed in white light from a full moon, but all the street-lamps had been switched off. It was quiet and deserted. Things were waiting to happen . . .

That's when I first heard the noise in the distance – the creak of a saddle and the whirr of some gears – getting closer and closer. I shivered with eager anticipation.

Billy Thomas, a fat boy who lived three doors down from my house, was riding his bicycle on the pavement, as he always did. He didn't seem to see the web I'd made and when he smacked into it his bike just kept on going, wobbling into the middle of the road where it fell over with a clatter. He caught one of his feet in the web and was stuck fast. Every time he tried to push himself off, another part of him

21

became entangled. I watched him until he was so tangled up that all he could do was move his eyes.

When I went up close to him he just looked at me, too scared to even speak.

He started to struggle, making the web hum in the process. He was puffing hard, his chubby little cheeks blowing in and out with all the effort he was making. But it didn't make any difference. I didn't feel in the slightest bit sorry for him.

I remember how natural it felt to crawl across the road and clamber up on to the web and how hungry I started to feel when I saw how fresh and tasty he looked.

When I reached out to touch one of his podgy arms the flesh dimpled and that made me lick my lips. That's when the begging look in his eyes went away and he started to scream.

"You've got to be quiet while I'm eating, Billy," I said sharply, "because it spoils my appetite."

Not long after that he stopped making a noise. But the strangest thing of all was that it wasn't a nightmare, because nightmares are frightening. It seemed quite natural.

I had trouble getting back to sleep after that because my arm started throbbing again, but in the end I just lay in my sleeping-bag, my head buried in the warm darkness. I must have dozed off because the next thing I remembered was Mark shaking me by the shoulder and saying it was time to get up. Sean was outside. He'd left the door open so daylight flooded in like daggers, making my eyes hurt.

I had another shock when I tried to get up: my neck was very sore. I don't mean it was just a bit stiff and uncomfortable, I mean it really hurt. It was so bad I had to swivel my whole body in order to look around.

When Sean saw this, he told me that I must have slept in a draught or something, but I knew that wasn't it. You see, I knew it had something to do with the spider bite because there were other funny things happening to me as well. My skin felt hard and brittle and I was sure I could feel hair, as tough as wire, sprouting out of my chest. Being twelve, I wanted chest-hair. I mean it was a sign I was growing up. But not like this. Not overnight! Something was changing in me, but I didn't know what it was and that was really scary!

When I dragged myself out of my sleeping-bag, Mark and Sean were outside making scrambled eggs. I couldn't face that sort of food for some reason. "Are you still feeling sick?" Sean asked when I said I didn't want any breakfast.

"No, I'm fine. I'll have something at lunchtime." When Mark asked about my arm, I said it was better and with a big effort, I managed to smile. I stayed out of the way while they ate and I didn't say anything about how funny I felt in case they thought I was whining. I knew the spider-bite had given me blood poisoning, but it wasn't as if I was at death's door: I just felt hot and shivery. All I really wanted to do was sleep . . .

As soon as breakfast was over we packed our things and headed off down the track. I think Sean and Mark knew something was wrong with me, but as I wasn't complaining, they didn't go on about it. I think they thought that because I'd survived this long, the worst was probably over.

As soon as we started walking I realized how shaky my legs felt and it was quite an effort to keep up with the other two, even though I knew they were walking much slower than they had done the day before.

I didn't like being out in the sun either. I felt exposed. I knew I had to keep looking up into the sky because that was where the danger was.

During our walk, when we'd been walking for an hour or so, I spotted a big black bird circling high in the air above us. I could see its long, pointy beak opening and shutting like a trap and it seemed to keep getting lower and lower all the time. I just knew it was watching me.

I tried to keep my eyes on it, but one moment it was

there and the next it had vanished. When I turned around to see where it had gone, it was swooping down behind me, its talons open like big claws, going straight for my head. That's when I panicked and cried out and threw my arms up to protect myself. I felt the wind from its wings as it went past and I ran to the shelter of some rocks and refused to come out until Mark and Sean threatened to leave me there.

We all laughed about it later, but inside I remained terrified because I knew that if that bird had swooped any lower, it would have been the end of me. We came across a small stream at noon. It was in a rocky gully and there were lots of shallow pools that were ideal for swimming in. Sean suggested we all go for a dip since we were making good time, and Mark agreed. They looked at me strangely when I explained that I didn't want to get in the water. They didn't say anything but I know they talked about it in private later on.

I sat down in the shade and for the first time since we had set out, I suddenly felt ravenously hungry. I had all sorts of food in my back-pack, but I didn't want any. I needed something else . . .

There was a termite nest near to where I was sitting and when the other two weren't looking I started picking up the termites and popping them into my mouth. I'd never realized before just how tasty they were, especially the small, young ones. They had a metallic bitter taste to them at first, but when you bit through the outer shells to suck out the soft parts inside, they were really sweet.

If Mark hadn't seen me and shouted out, "Hey, Jo, what are you eating?" I think I could have happily sat there all day.

I jumped up, feeling embarrassed and guilty.

"Nothing," I answered, too quickly.

There was a suspicious look on his face as he walked over to me. "I thought for a second you were eating bugs," he said.

I felt a terrible desire to dart away from him and

get back into the shade where it was safer, but I managed to control myself.

"I was eating a biscuit. A few crumbs fell on the rock."

He relaxed then and when Sean came over Mark told him what he'd said to me and they made a joke of the whole thing. While we were talking my eyes went funny. One minute I was looking at them and everything was normal and the next all the colours had changed. It was as if I was peering through one of those heat-sensitive, infra-red scopes which soldiers use at night.

Mark and Sean were bright red, especially round the face, the rocks were pink and the shady areas were a purply-blue. That's when my mouth went dry. I couldn't speak because I was shaking so much. I'd never been so scared in all my life and I didn't think I could go any further. Then, without warning, I could see properly again.

I didn't think Sean and Mark would have noticed anything but when I looked at them I could see they had worried looks on their faces.

"I just had a dizzy spell," I explained then walked away because I didn't want to talk to them. You see, there had been something else. When I'd put my hand on the rock to get up, I could tell where the termites had been running. But surely that was impossible?

People can't smell through their fingers, can they? Only spiders can . . .

I think it was then that I realized for the first time that I was changing.

But I didn't say anything to the others, even though my heart was beating fast and I was frightened to be out of the shadows. All I wanted to do was to get to the next hut where I could rest again, so I forced myself to go out into the sun and I started off down the trail as if everything was all right.

We carried on walking but by mid-afternoon my legs were so stiff I could hardly bend them. By this time we weren't talking that much and sometimes they'd get ahead of me and then have to wait while I caught up. They'd be angry then and want to say something to me but were kind enough not to. I wanted to tell them something was happening to me, that I was feeling weird and moving as fast as I could. But when I tried to speak, my voice sounded high-pitched and twittery and I didn't think they'd understand, so in the end I just kept quiet.

We got to the second hut around five o'clock. We should have got there about three hours earlier but I know I slowed us all down.

After we'd put our sleeping-bags down, I found I couldn't straighten my back properly and I knew I'd have to get rid of my back-pack. But at the time I thought that was the least of my problems. I couldn't carry it and I couldn't really dump it, but I didn't want it any more. My jeans and T-shirt were also becoming uncomfortable and pressing too tightly against my skin. I needed to get rid of them. But walking around naked in a nature reserve was not the sort of thing a normal person did. All I wanted to do was get away from the track and find a dark place to hide in the undergrowth.

I managed to force some baked beans and viennas down at supper, but afterwards I had to go off into the bushes and make myself sick because I felt as if I'd been poisoned. While I was away from the hut I managed to find a few grubs, which I gulped down. They made me feel much better and took the edge off my hunger.

Monday

I lay in my sleeping-bag wide awake, long after Mark and Sean had gone to sleep. Even though it was pitch black in the hut I could see both of them quite clearly because they were actually glowing. A bright red at first, then after they had been sleeping soundly for some time, they turned a kind of deep maroon.

I kept drifting in and out of sleep, but I couldn't rest properly. I was dreaming about spiders and I knew I couldn't go on the next day, not in the light anyway. That would kill me. Mark and Sean wouldn't understand of course. They'd just think I'd gone off my head, suffering from blood poisoning, or something. They wouldn't be able to accept that I was . . . changing.

It was just before dawn that I realized I had to get away and hide. Just as the first rays of sun were appearing in the sky, I crept out of my sleeping-bag, rolled it up so that I could carry it with me and quietly sneaked out of the hut.

I headed off into the wild lands, away from the river and as far as possible from tracks that any hikers might follow. The trouble was, I could only move very slowly. Sometimes I had to walk sideways and every movement was an effort because all I really wanted to do was lie down and sleep.

Just as it was getting dark, I managed to find a crack beneath an overhang in the valley wall. Luckily, it was big enough for me to squeeze myself into. I laid out my sleeping-bag, clambered inside, and closed my eyes.

I was very hot and I vaguely remember waking up hours later and hearing Mark calling to me in the distance. He said I had to come back and that Sean had gone to get some help, but I didn't answer, because all I wanted to do was stay in the shady dark until the change in me was complete.

I felt hungry all the time and I knew I'd have to weave a web so that I could catch the flies and crawling things that came into my lair. I think I also heard a field mouse or a mole moving around but although I stayed very, very quiet, it didn't come near enough for me to get hold of it.

I think it was just before dawn the next day that I heard the buzzing sound far off in the distance. The noise kept getting closer and I could feel the air vibrate. I was scared because I could tell the insects were coming to get me. The next thing I knew, a tall black shape like a monstrous ant with a huge domed head was standing over me, twittering away. Then I felt a sharp pain in my arm and everything went black again . . .

Later, I remember floating in a white universe, while all around me there were machines that wheezed and clicked. Eventually, the light faded as night-time swiftly approached. Sometime during the darkness I heard a shoe squeak on the rubber floor, then my father's whispered voice.

"You were bitten by a spider," he said, before he faded from me.

Eventually, the light returned and he was still speaking but this time I was at the bottom of a deep well and I could see his face silhouetted in the bright sunlight above me.

"You had a terrible fever and became delirious on the first night," he was saying. "Sean had to run for help. They had to bring you off the mountain in a helicopter and then transport you to this hospital."

I couldn't understand how my father had become so confused.

"No, Dad, you've got it all wrong. We made it to the second hut . . ." I tried to say, but a swollen tongue made a meaningless jumble of my words. Yet he seemed to understand all the same because I remember he squeezed my hand.

"You're going to be all right now, son," he said. "But there was no second day, nor a second hut, except in your head, of course . . ."

The Veldt

Ray Bradbury

"George, I wish you'd look at the nursery."

"What's wrong with it?"

"I don't know."

"Well, then."

"I just want you to look at it, is all, or call a psychologist in to look at it."

"What would a psychologist want with a nursery?"

"You know very well what he'd want." His wife paused in the middle of the kitchen and watched the stove busy humming to itself, making supper for four.

"It's just that the nursery is different now than it was."

"All right, let's have a look."

They walked down the hall of their sound-proofed, Happy-life Home, which had cost them thirty thousand dollars to install, this house which clothed and fed and rocked them to sleep and played and sang and was good to them. Their approach sensitized a switch somewhere and the nursery light flicked on when they came within ten feet of it. Similarly, behind them, in the halls, lights went on and off as they left them behind, with a soft automaticity.

"Well," said George Hadley.

They stood on the thatched floor of the nursery. It was forty feet across by forty feet long and thirty feet high; it had cost half as much again as the rest of the house. "But nothing's too good for our children," George had said.

The nursery was silent. It was empty as a jungle glade at hot high noon. The walls were blank and two-dimensional. Now, as George and Lydia Hadley stood in the centre of the room, the walls began to purr and recede into crystalline distance, it seemed, and presently an African veldt appeared, in three dimensions, on all sides, in colour, reproduced to the final pebble and bit of straw. The ceiling above them became a deep sky with a hot yellow sun.

George Hadley felt the perspiration start on his brow.

"Let's get out of this sun," he said. "This is a little too real. But I don't see anything wrong."

"Wait a moment, you'll see," said his wife.

Now the hidden odorophonics were beginning to

blow a wind of odour at the two people in the middle of the baked veldtland. The hot straw smell of lion grass, the cool green smell of the hidden water-hole, the great rusty smell of animals, the smell of dust like a red paprika in the hot air. And now the sounds: the thump of distant antelope feet on grassy sod, the papery rustling of vultures. A shadow passed through the sky. The shadow flickered on George Hadley's upturned, sweating features.

"Filthy creatures," he heard his wife say.

"The vultures."

"You see, there are the lions, far over, that way.

Now they're on their way to the water-hole. They've just been eating," said Lydia. "I don't know what."

"Some animal." George Hadley put his hand up to shield off the burning light from his squinted eyes. "A zebra or a baby giraffe, maybe."

"Are you *sure*?" His wife sounded peculiarly tense.

"No, it's a little late to be *sure*," he said, amused. "Nothing over there I can see but cleaned bone and the vultures dropping for what's left."

"Did you hear that scream?" she asked.

"No."

"About a minute ago?"

"Sorry, no."

The lions were coming. And again George Hadley was filled with admiration for the mechanical genius who had conceived this room. A miracle of efficiency selling for an absurdly low price. Every home should have one. Oh, occasionally they frightened you with their clinical accuracy, they startled you, gave you a twinge, but most of the time what fun for everyone, not only your own son and daughter but for yourself when you felt like a quick jaunt to a foreign land, a quick change of scenery. Well, here it was!

And here were the lions now, fifteen feet away, so real, so feverishly and startlingly real that you could feel the prickling fur on your hand, and your mouth was stuffed with the dusty upholstery smell of their heated pelts, and the yellow of them was in your eyes like the yellow of an exquisite French tapestry, the yellows of lions and summer grass, and the sound of the matted lion lungs exhaling on the silent noontide, and the smell of meat from the panting, dripping mouths.

The lions stood looking at George and Lydia Hadley with terrible green-yellow eyes.

"Watch out!" screamed Lydia.

The lions came running at them.

Lydia bolted and ran. Instinctively, George sprang after her. Outside, in the hall, with the door slammed, he was laughing and she was crying, and they both stood appalled at the other's reaction.

"George!"

"Lydia! Oh, my dear poor sweet Lydia!"

"They almost got us!"

"Walls, Lydia, remember; crystal walls, that's all they are. Oh, they look real, I must admit – Africa in your parlour – but it's all dimensional super-reactionary, super-sensitive colour film and mental tape film behind glass screens. It's all odorophonics and sonics, Lydia. Here's my handkerchief."

"I'm afraid." She came to him and put her body against him and cried steadily. "Did you see? Did you feel? It's too real."

"Now, Lydia . . ."

"You've got to tell Wendy and Peter not to read any more on Africa."

"Of course – of course." He patted her.

"Promise?"

"Sure."

"And lock the nursery for a few days until I get my nerves settled."

"You know how difficult Peter is about that. When I punished him a month ago by locking the nursery for even a few hours – the tantrum he threw! And Wendy too. They live for the nursery."

"It's got to be locked, that's all there is to it."

"All right." Reluctantly he locked the huge door. "You've been working too hard. You need a rest."

"I don't know – I don't know," she said, blowing her nose, and sitting down in a chair that immediately began to rock and comfort her. "Maybe I don't have enough to do. Maybe I have time to think too much. Why don't we shut the whole house off for a few days and take a vacation?"

"You mean you want to fry my eggs for me?"

"Yes." She nodded.

"And darn my socks?"

"Yes." A frantic, watery-eyed nodding.

"And sweep the house?"

"Yes, yes – oh yes!"

"But I thought that's why we bought this house, so

we wouldn't have to do anything?"

"That's just it. I feel like I don't belong here. The house is wife and mother now and nursemaid. Can I compete with an African veldt? Can I give a bath and scrub the children as efficiently or quickly as the automatic scrub bath can? I cannot. And it isn't just me. It's you. You've been awfully nervous lately."

"I suppose I have been smoking too much."

"You look as if you didn't know what to do with yourself in this house, either. You smoke a little more every morning and drink a little more every afternoon and need a little more sedative every night. You're beginning to feel unnecessary too."

"Am I?" He paused and tried to feel into himself to see what was really there.

"Oh, George!" She looked beyond him, at the nursery door. "Those lions can't get out of there, can they?"

He looked at the door and saw it tremble as if something had jumped against it from the other side.

"Of course not," he said.

At dinner they ate alone, for Wendy and Peter were at a special plastic carnival across town and had televised home to say they'd be late, to go ahead eating. So George Hadley, bemused, sat watching the dining-room table produce warm dishes of food from its mechanical interior.

"We forgot the ketchup," he said.

"Sorry," said a small voice within the table, and ketchup appeared.

As for the nursery, thought George Hadley, it won't hurt for the children to be locked out of it a while. Too much of anything isn't good for anyone. And it was clearly indicated that the children had been spending a little too much time on Africa. That *sun*. He could feel it on his neck, still, like a hot paw. And the *lions*. And the smell of blood. Remarkable how the nursery caught the telepathic emanations of the children's minds and created life to fill their every desire. The children thought lions, and there were lions. The children thought zebras, and there were zebras. Sun – sun. Giraffes – giraffes. Death and death.

That *last*. He chewed tastelessly on the meat that the table had cut for him. Death thoughts. They were awfully young, Wendy and Peter, for death thoughts. Or, no, you were never too young, really. Long before you knew what death was you were wishing it on someone else. When you were two years old you were shooting people with cap pistols.

But this – the long, hot African veldt – the awful death in the jaws of a lion. And repeated again and again.

"Where are you going?"

He didn't answer Lydia. Preoccupied, he let the lights glow softly on ahead of him, extinguish behind him as he padded to the nursery door. He listened against it. Far away, a lion roared.

He unlocked the door and opened it. Just before he stepped inside, he heard a faraway scream. And then another roar from the lions, which subsided quickly.

He stepped into Africa. How many times in the last year had he opened this door and found Wonderland, Alice, the Mock Turtle, or Aladdin and his Magical Lamp, or Jack Pumpkinhead of Oz, or Dr Dolittle, or the cow jumping over a very real-appearing moon – all the delightful contraptions of a make-believe world. How often had he seen Pegasus flying in the sky ceiling, or seen fountains of red fireworks, or heard angel voices singing. But now, this yellow hot Africa, this bake oven with murder in the heat. Perhaps Lydia was right. Perhaps they needed a little vacation from the fantasy which was growing a bit too real for ten-year-old children. It was all right to exercise one's mind with gymnastic fantasies, but when the lively child mind settled on one pattern . . .? It seemed that, at a distance, for the past month, he had heard lions roaring, and smelled their strong odour seeping as far away as his study door. But, being busy, he had paid it no attention.

George Hadley stood on the African grassland alone. The lions looked up from their feeding, watching him. The only flaw to the illusion was the open door through which he could see his wife, far down the dark hall, like a framed picture, eating her dinner abstractedly.

"Go away," he said to the lions.

They did not go.

He knew the principle of the room exactly. You sent out your thoughts. Whatever you thought would appear.

"Let's have Aladdin and his lamp," he snapped.

The veldtland remained, the lions remained.

"Come on, room! I demand Aladdin!" he said.

Nothing happened. The lions mumbled in their baked pelts.

"Aladdin!"

He went back to dinner. "The fool room's out of order," he said. "It won't respond."

"Or—"

"Or what?"

"Or it *can't* respond," said Lydia, "because the children have thought about Africa and lions and killing so many days that the room's in a rut."

"Could be."

"Or Peter's set it to remain that way."

"*Set* it?"

"He may have got into the machinery and fixed something."

"Peter doesn't know machinery."

"He's a wise one for ten. That IQ of his—"

"Nevertheless—"

"Hello, Mum. Hello, Dad."

The Hadleys turned. Wendy and Peter were coming in the front door, cheeks like peppermint candy, eyes like bright blue agate marbles, a smell of ozone on their jumpers from their trip in the helicopter.

"You're just in time for supper," said both parents.

"We're full of strawberry ice cream and hot dogs," said the children, holding hands. "But we'll sit and watch."

"Yes, come tell us about the nursery," said George Hadley.

The brother and sister blinked at him and then at each other. "Nursery?"

"All about Africa and everything," said the father with false joviality.

"I don't understand," said Peter.

"Your mother and I were just travelling through Africa with rod and reel; Tom Swift and his Electric Lion," said George Hadley.

"There's no Africa in the nursery," said Peter simply.

43

"Oh, come now, Peter. We know better."

"I don't remember any Africa," said Peter to Wendy. "Do you?"

"No."

"Run and see and come tell."

She obeyed.

"Wendy, come back here!" said George Hadley, but she was gone. The house lights followed her like a flock of fireflies. Too late, he realized he had forgotten to lock the nursery door after his last inspection.

"Wendy'll look and come tell us," said Peter.

"She doesn't have to tell *me*. I've seen it."

"I'm sure you're mistaken, Father."

"I'm not, Peter. Come along now."

But Wendy was back. "It's not Africa," she said breathlessly.

"We'll see about this," said George Hadley, and they all walked down the hall together and opened the nursery door.

There was a green, lovely forest, a lovely river, a purple mountain, high voices singing, and Rima, lovely and mysterious, lurking in the trees with colourful flights of butterflies, like animated bouquets, lingering in her long hair. The African veldtland was gone. The lions were gone. Only Rima was here now, singing a song so beautiful that it brought tears to your eyes.

George Hadley looked in at the changed scene. "Go to bed," he said to the children.

They opened their mouths.

"You heard me," he said.

They went off to the air closet, where a wind sucked them like brown leaves up the flue to their slumber rooms.

George Hadley walked through the singing glade and picked up something that lay in the corner near where the lions had been. He walked slowly back to his wife.

"What is that?" she asked.

"An old wallet of mine," he said.

He showed it to her. The smell of hot grass was on it and the smell of a lion. There were drops of saliva on it, it had been chewed, and there were blood smears on both sides.

He closed the nursery door and locked it, tight.

In the middle of the night he was still awake and he knew his wife was awake. "Do you think Wendy changed it?" she said at last, in the dark room.

"Of course."

"Made it from a veldt into a forest and put Rima there instead of lions?"

"Yes."

45

"Why?"

"I don't know. But it's staying locked until I find out."

"How did your wallet get there?"

"I don't know anything," he said, "except that I'm beginning to be sorry we bought that room for the children. If children are neurotic at all, a room like that—"

"It's supposed to help them work off their neuroses in a healthful way."

"I'm starting to wonder." He stared at the ceiling.

"We've given the children everything they ever wanted. Is this our reward – secrecy, disobedience?"

"Who was it said, 'Children are like carpets, they should be stepped on occasionally'? We've never lifted a hand. They're insufferable – let's admit it. They come and go when they like; they treat us as if *we* were offspring. They're spoiled and we're spoiled."

"They've been acting funny ever since you forbade them to take the rocket to New York a few months ago."

"They're not old enough to do that alone, I explained."

"Nevertheless, I've noticed they've been decidedly cool towards us since."

"I think I'll have David McClean come tomorrow

46

morning to have a look at Africa."

"But it's not Africa now, it's Green Mansions country and Rima."

"I have a feeling it'll be Africa again before then."

A moment later they heard the screams.

Two screams. Two people screaming from downstairs. And then a roar of lions.

"Wendy and Peter aren't in their rooms," said his wife.

He lay in his bed with his beating heart. "No," he said. "They've broken into the nursery."

"Those screams – they sound familiar."

"Do they?"

"Yes, awfully."

And although their beds tried very hard, the two adults couldn't be rocked to sleep for another hour. A smell of cats was in the night air.

"Father?" said Peter.

"Yes."

Peter looked at his shoes. He never looked at his father any more, nor at his mother. "You aren't going to lock up the nursery for good, are you?"

"That all depends."

"On what?" snapped Peter.

"On you and your sister. If you intersperse this Africa with a little variety – oh, Sweden, perhaps, or Denmark or China—"

"I thought we were free to play as we wished."

"You are, within reasonable bounds."

"What's wrong with Africa, Father?"

"Oh, so now you admit you have been conjuring up Africa, do you?"

"I wouldn't want the nursery locked up," said Peter coldly. "Ever."

"Matter of fact, we're thinking of turning the whole house off for about a month. Live sort of a carefree one-for-all existence."

"That sounds dreadful! Would I have to tie my own shoes instead of letting the shoe-tier do it? And brush my own teeth and comb my hair and give myself a bath?"

"It would be fun for a change, don't you think?"

"No, it would be horrid. I didn't like it when you took out the picture painter last month."

"That's because I wanted you to learn to paint all by yourself, son."

"I don't want to do anything but look and listen and smell; what else is there to do?"

"All right, go play in Africa."

"Will you shut off the house sometime soon?"

"We're considering it."

"I don't think you'd better consider it any more, Father."

"I won't have any threats from my son!"

"Very well." And Peter strolled off to the nursery.

"Am I on time?" said David McClean.

"Breakfast?" asked George Hadley.

"Thanks, had some. What's the trouble?"

"David, you're a psychologist."

"I should hope so."

"Well, then, have a look at our nursery. You saw it a year ago when you dropped by; did you notice anything peculiar about it then?"

"Can't say I did; the usual violences, a tendency towards a slight paranoia here or there, usual in children because they feel persecuted by parents constantly, but, oh, really nothing."

They walked down the hall. "I locked the nursery up," explained the father, "and the children broke back into it during the night. I let them stay so they could form the patterns for you to see."

There was a terrible screaming from the nursery.

"There it is," said George Hadley. "See what you make of it."

They walked in on the children without rapping.

The screams had faded. The lions were feeding.

"Run outside a moment, children," said George Hadley. "No, don't change the mental combination. Leave the walls as they are. Get!"

With the children gone, the two men stood studying the lions clustered at a distance, eating with great relish whatever it was they had caught.

"I wish I knew what it was," said George Hadley. "Sometimes I can almost see. Do you think if I brought high-powered binoculars here and—"

David McClean laughed dryly. "Hardly." He turned to study all four walls. "How long has this been going on?"

"A little over a month."

"It certainly doesn't feel good."

"I want facts, not feelings."

"My dear George, a psychologist never saw a fact in his life. He only hears about feelings; vague things. This doesn't feel good, I tell you. Trust my hunches and my instincts, I have a nose for something bad. This is very bad. My advice to you is to have the whole damn room torn down and your children brought to me every day during the next year for treatment."

"Is it that bad?"

"I'm afraid so. One of the original uses of these nurseries was so that we could study the patterns left on the walls by the child's mind, study at our leisure, and help the child. In this case, however, the room has become a channel towards – destructive thoughts, instead of a release away from them."

50

"Didn't you sense this before?"

"I sensed only that you had spoiled your children more than most. And now you're letting them down in some way. What way?"

"I wouldn't let them go to New York."

"What else?"

"I've taken a few machines from the house and threatened them, a month ago, with closing up the nursery unless they did their homework. I did close it for a few days to show I meant business."

"Aha!"

"Does that mean anything?"

"Everything. Where before they had a Santa Claus now they have a Scrooge. Children prefer Santas. You've let this room and this house replace you and your wife in your children's affections. This room is their mother and father, far more important in their lives than their real parents. And now you've come along and want to shut it off. No wonder there's hatred there. You can feel it coming out of the sky. Feel that sun. George, you'll have to change your life. Like too many others, you've built it around creature comforts. Why, you'd starve tomorrow if something went wrong in your kitchen. You wouldn't know how to tap an egg. Nevertheless, turn everything off. Start new. It'll take time. But we'll make good children out of bad in a year, wait and see."

"But won't the shock be too much for the children, shutting the room up abruptly, for good?"

"I don't want them going any deeper into this, that's all."

The lions were finished with their red feast.

The lions were standing on the edge of the clearing watching the two men.

"Now *I'm* feeling persecuted," said McClean. "Let's get out of here. I never have cared for these damned rooms. Make me nervous."

"The lions look real, don't they?" said George Hadley. "I don't suppose there's any way—"

"What?"

"– that they could *become* real?"

"Not that I know."

"Some flaw in the machinery, a tampering or something?"

"No."

They went to the door.

"I don't imagine the room will like being turned off," said the father.

"Nothing ever likes to die – even a room."

"I wonder if it hates me for wanting to switch it off?"

"Paranoia is thick around here today," said David McClean. "You can follow it like a spoor. Hello." He bent and picked up a bloody scarf. "This yours?"

"No." George Hadley's face was rigid. "It belongs to Lydia."

They went to the fuse-box together and threw the switch that killed the nursery.

The two children were in hysterics. They screamed and pranced and threw things. They yelled and sobbed and swore and jumped at the furniture.

"You can't do that to the nursery, you can't!"

"Now, children."

The children flung themselves on to a couch, weeping.

"George," said Lydia Hadley, "turn on the nursery, just for a few moments. You can't be so abrupt."

"No."

"You can't be so cruel."

"Lydia, it's off, and it stays off. And the whole damn house dies as of here and now. The more I see of the mess we've put ourselves in, the more it sickens me. We've been contemplating our mechanical, electronic navels for too long. My God, how we need a breath of honest air!"

And he marched about the house turning off the voice clocks, the stoves, the heaters, the shoe-shiners, the shoe-lacers, the body-scrubbers and swabbers and massagers, and every other machine he could put his hand to.

The house was full of dead bodies, it seemed. It felt like a mechanical cemetery. So silent. None of the humming hidden energy of machines waiting to function at the tap of a button.

"Don't let them do it!" wailed Peter at the ceiling, as if he was talking to the house, the nursery. "Don't let Father kill everything." He turned to his father. "Oh, I hate you!"

"Insults won't get you anywhere."

"I wish you were dead!"

"We were, for a long while. Now we're going to really start living. Instead of being handled and massaged, we're going to live."

Wendy was still crying and Peter joined her again. "Just a moment, just one moment, just another moment of nursery," they wailed.

"Oh, George," said the wife, "it can't hurt."

"All right – all right, if they'll only just shut up. One minute, mind you, and then off for ever."

"Daddy, Daddy, Daddy!" sang the children, smiling with wet faces.

"And then we're going on a vacation. David McClean is coming back in half an hour to help us move out and get to the airport. I'm going to dress. You turn the nursery on for a minute, Lydia, just a minute, mind you."

And the three of them went babbling off while he let himself be vacuumed upstairs through the air flue and set about dressing himself. A minute later Lydia appeared.

"I'll be glad when we get away," she sighed.

"Did you leave them in the nursery?"

"I wanted to dress too. Oh, that horrid Africa. What can they see in it?"

"Well, in five minutes we'll be on our way to Iowa. Lord, how did we ever get in this house? What prompted us to buy a nightmare?"

"Pride, money, foolishness."

"I think we'd better get downstairs before those kids get engrossed with those damned beasts again."

Just then they heard the children calling, "Daddy, Mummy, come quick – quick!"

They went downstairs in the air flue and ran down the hall. The children were nowhere in sight. "Wendy? Peter!"

They ran into the nursery. The veldtland was empty save for the lions waiting, looking at them. "Peter, Wendy?"

The door slammed.

"Wendy, Peter!"

George Hadley and his wife whirled and ran back to the door.

"Open the door!" cried George Hadley, trying the

knob. "Why, they've locked it from the outside! Peter!" He beat at the door. "Open up!"

He heard Peter's voice outside, against the door.

"Don't let them switch off the nursery and the house," he was saying.

Mr and Mrs George Hadley beat at the door. "Now, don't be ridiculous, children. It's time to go. Mr McClean'll be here in a minute and . . ."

And then they heard the sounds.

The lions on three sides of them, in the yellow veldt grass, padding through the dry straw, rumbling and roaring in their throats.

The lions.

Mr Hadley looked at his wife and they turned and looked back at the beasts edging slowly forward, crouching, tails stiff.

Mr and Mrs Hadley screamed.

And suddenly they realized why those other screams had sounded familiar.

"Well, here I am," said David McClean in the nursery doorway. "Oh, hello." He stared at the two children seated in the centre of the open glade eating a little picnic lunch. Beyond them was the water-hole and the yellow veldtland; above was the hot sun. He began to perspire. "Where are your father and mother?"

The children looked up and smiled. "Oh, they'll be here directly."

"Good, we must get going." At a distance Mr McClean saw the lions fighting and clawing and then quieting down to feed in silence under the shady trees.

He squinted at the lions with his hands up to his eyes.

Now the lions were done feeding. They moved to the water-hole to drink.

A shadow flickered over Mr McClean's hot face. Many shadows flickered. The vultures were dropping down the blazing sky.

"A cup of tea?" asked Wendy in the silence.

The Surgeon

Roald Dahl

"**Y**ou have done extraordinarily well," Robert Sandy said, seating himself behind the desk. "It's altogether a splendid recovery. I don't think there's any need for you to come and see me any more."

The patient finished putting on his clothes and said to the surgeon, "May I speak to you, please, for another moment?"

"Of course you may," Robert Sandy said. "Take a seat."

The man sat down opposite the surgeon and leaned forward, placing his hands, palms downward, on the top of the desk. "I suppose you still refuse to take a fee?" he said.

"I've never taken one yet and I don't propose to change my ways at this time of life," Robert Sandy told him pleasantly. "I work entirely for the National Health Service and they pay me a very fair salary."

Robert Sandy MA, M. CHIR, FRCS, had been at the Radcliffe Infirmary in Oxford for eighteen years and he was now 52 years old, with a wife and three grown-up children. Unlike many of his colleagues, he did not hanker after fame and riches. He was basically a simple man utterly devoted to his profession.

It was now seven weeks since his patient, a university undergraduate, had been rushed into Casualty by ambulance after a nasty car accident in the Banbury Road not far from the hospital. He was suffering from massive abdominal injuries and he had lost consciousness. When the call came through from Casualty for an emergency surgeon, Robert Sandy was up in his office having a cup of tea after a fairly arduous morning's work which had included a gall-bladder, a prostate and a total colostomy, but for some reason he happened to be the only general surgeon available at that moment. He took one more sip of his tea, then walked straight back into the operating theatre and started scrubbing up all over again.

After three and a half hours on the operating table, the patient was still alive and Robert Sandy had done everything he could to save his life. The next day, to the surgeon's considerable surprise, the man was showing signs that he was going to survive. In addition, his mind was lucid and he was speaking coherently. It was only then, on the morning after the operation, that Robert Sandy began to realize that he had an important person on his hands. Three dignified gentlemen from the Saudi Arabian Embassy, including the Ambassador himself, came into the hospital and the first thing they wanted was to call in all manner of celebrated surgeons from Harley Street to advise on the case. The patient, with bottles suspended all round his bed and tubes running into many parts of his body, shook his head and murmured something in Arabic to the Ambassador.

"He says he wants only you to look after him," the Ambassador said to Robert Sandy.

"You are very welcome to call in anyone else you choose for consultation," Robert Sandy said.

"Not if he doesn't want us to," the Ambassador said. "He says you have saved his life and he has absolute faith in you. We must respect his wishes."

The Ambassador then told Robert Sandy that his patient was none other than a prince of royal blood. In other words, he was one of the many sons of the present king of Saudi Arabia.

A few days later, when the Prince was off the danger list, the Embassy tried once again to persuade him to make a change. They wanted him to be moved to a far more luxurious hospital that catered only for private patients, but the Prince would have none of it. "I stay here," he said, "with the surgeon who saved my life."

Robert Sandy was touched by the confidence his patient was putting in him, and throughout the long weeks of recovery, he did his best to ensure that this confidence was not misplaced.

And now, in the consulting-room, the Prince was saying, "I do wish you would allow me to pay you for all you have done, Mr Sandy." The young man had spent three years at Oxford and he knew very well that in England a surgeon was always addressed as "Mister" and not "Doctor". "Please let me pay you, Mr Sandy," he said.

Robert Sandy shook his head. "I'm sorry," he answered, "but I still have to say no. It's just a personal rule of mine and I won't break it."

"But dash it all, you saved my life," the Prince said, tapping the palms of his hands on the desk.

"I did no more than any other competent surgeon would have done," Robert Sandy said.

The Prince took his hands off the desk and clasped them on his lap. "All right, Mr Sandy, even though you refuse a fee, there is surely no reason why my father should not give you a small present to show his gratitude."

Robert Sandy shrugged his shoulders. Grateful

patients quite often gave him a case of whisky or a dozen bottles of wine and he accepted these things gracefully. He never expected them, but he was awfully pleased when they arrived. It was a nice way of saying thank you.

The Prince took from his jacket pocket a small pouch made of black velvet and he pushed it across the desk. "My father," he said, "has asked me to tell you how enormously indebted he is to you for what you have done. He told me that whether you took a fee or not, I was to make sure you accepted this little gift."

Robert Sandy looked suspiciously at the black pouch, but he made no move to take it.

"My father," the Prince went on, "said also to tell you that in his eyes my life is without price and that nothing on earth can repay you adequately for having saved it. This is simply a . . . what shall we call it . . . a present for your next birthday. A small birthday present."

"He shouldn't give me anything," Robert Sandy said.

"Look at it, please," the Prince said.

Rather gingerly, the surgeon picked up the pouch and loosened the silk thread at the opening. When he tipped it upside down, there was a flash of brilliant light as something ice-white dropped on to the plain

wooden desk-top. The stone was about the size of a
cashew nut or a bit larger, perhaps three-quarters of
an inch long from end to end, and it was pear shaped,
with a very sharp point at the narrow end. Its many
facets glimmered and sparkled in the most wonderful
way.

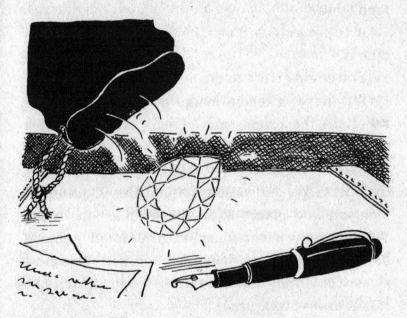

"Good gracious me," Robert Sandy said, looking at
it but not yet touching it. "What is it?"

"It's a diamond," the Prince said. "Pure white. It's
not especially large, but the colour is good."

"I really can't accept a present like this," Robert
Sandy said. "No, it wouldn't be right. It must be quite
valuable."

The Prince smiled at him. "I must tell you something, Mr Sandy," he said. "Nobody refuses a gift from the King. It would be a terrible insult. It has never been done."

Robert Sandy looked back at the Prince. "Oh dear," he said. "You *are* making it awkward for me, aren't you?"

"It is not awkward at all," the Prince said. "Just take it."

"You could give it to the hospital."

"We have already made a donation to the hospital," the Prince said. "Please take it, not just for my father, but for me as well."

"You are very kind," Robert Sandy said. "All right, then. But I feel quite embarrassed." He picked up the diamond and placed it in the palm of one hand. "There's never been a diamond in our family before," he said. "Gosh, it is beautiful, isn't it. You must please convey my thanks to His Majesty and tell him I shall always treasure it."

"You don't actually have to hang on to it," the Prince said. "My father would not be in the least offended if you were to sell it. Who knows, one day you might need a little pocket-money."

"I don't think I shall sell it," Robert Sandy said. "It is too lovely. Perhaps I shall have it made into a pendant for my wife."

"What a nice idea," the Prince said, getting up from his chair. "And please remember what I told you before. You and your wife are invited to my country at any time. My father would be happy to welcome you both."

"That's very good of him," Robert Sandy said. "I won't forget."

When the Prince had gone, Robert Sandy picked up the diamond again and examined it with total fascination. It was dazzling in its beauty, and as he moved it gently from side to side in his palm, one facet after the other caught the light from the window and flashed brilliantly with blue and pink and gold. He glanced at his watch. It was ten minutes past three. An idea had come to him. He picked up the telephone and asked his secretary if there was anything else urgent for him to do that afternoon. If there wasn't, he told her, then he thought he might leave early.

"There's nothing that can't wait until Monday," the secretary said, sensing that for once this most hard-working of men had some special reason for wanting to go.

"I've got a few things of my own I'd very much like to do."

"Off you go, Mr Sandy," she said. "Try to get some rest over the weekend. I'll see you on Monday."

In the hospital car park, Robert Sandy unchained his bicycle, mounted and rode out on to the Woodstock Road. He still cycled to work every day unless the weather was foul. It kept him in shape and it also meant his wife could have the car. There was nothing odd about that. Half the population of Oxford rode on bicycles. He turned into the Woodstock Road and headed for The High. The only good jeweller in town had his shop in The High, halfway up on the right and he was called H. F. Gold. It said so above the window, and most people knew that H stood for Harry. Harry Gold had been there a long time, but Robert had only been inside once, years ago, to buy a small bracelet for his daughter as a confirmation present.

He parked his bike against the kerb outside the shop and went in. A woman behind the counter asked if she could help him.

"Is Mr Gold in?" Robert Sandy said.

"Yes, he is."

"I would like to see him privately for a few minutes, if I may. My name is Sandy."

"Just a minute, please." The woman disappeared through a door at the back, but in thirty seconds she returned and said, "Will you come this way, please."

Robert Sandy walked into a large untidy office in which a small, oldish man was seated behind a

66

partner's desk. He wore a grey goatee beard and steel spectacles, and he stood up as Robert approached him.

"Mr Gold, my name is Robert Sandy. I am a surgeon at the Radcliffe. I wonder if you can help me."

"I'll do my best, Mr Sandy. Please sit down."

"Well, it's an odd story," Robert Sandy said. "I recently operated on one of the Saudi princes. He's in his third year at Magdalen and he'd been involved in a nasty car accident. And now he has given me, or rather his father has given me, a fairly wonderful-looking diamond."

"Good gracious me," Mr Gold said. "How very exciting."

"I didn't want to accept it, but I'm afraid it was more or less forced on me."

"And you would like me to look at it?"

"Yes, I would. You see, I haven't the faintest idea whether it's worth five hundred pounds or five thousand, and it's only sensible that I should know roughly what the value is."

"Of course you should," Harry Gold said. "I'll be glad to help you. Doctors at the Radcliffe have helped *me* a great deal over the years."

Robert Sandy took the black pouch out of his pocket and placed it on the desk. Harry Gold opened the pouch and tipped the diamond into his hand. As the stone fell into his palm, there was a moment when the old man appeared to freeze. His whole body became motionless as he sat there staring at the brilliant shining thing that lay before him. Slowly, he stood up. He walked over to the window and held the stone so that daylight fell upon it. He turned it over with one finger. He didn't say a word. His expression never changed. Still holding the diamond, he returned to his desk and from a drawer he took out a single sheet of clean white paper. He made a loose fold in the paper and placed the diamond in the fold. Then he returned to the window and stood there for a full minute studying the diamond that lay in the fold of paper.

"I am looking at the colour," he said at last. "That's the first thing to do. One always does that against a fold of white paper and preferably in a north light."

"Is that a north light?"

"Yes, it is. This stone is a wonderful colour, Mr Sandy. As fine a D colour as I've ever seen. In the trade, the very best quality white is called a D colour. In some places it's called a River. That's mostly in Scandinavia. A layman would call it a Blue White."

"It doesn't look very blue to me," Robert Sandy said.

"The purest whites always contain a trace of blue," Harry Gold said. "That's why in the old days they always put a blue-bag into the washing water. It made the clothes whiter."

"Ah yes, of course."

Harry Gold went back to his desk and took out from another drawer a sort of hooded magnifying glass. "This is a ten-times loupe," he said, holding it up.

"What did you call it?"

"A loupe. It is simply a jeweller's magnifier. With this, I can examine the stone for imperfections."

Back once again at the window, Harry Gold began a minute examination of the diamond through the ten-times loupe, holding the paper with the stone on it in one hand and the loupe in the other. This process took maybe four minutes. Robert Sandy watched him and kept quiet.

"So far as I can see," Harry Gold said, "it is completely flawless. It really is a most lovely stone. The quality is superb and the cutting is very fine, though definitely not modern."

"Approximately how many facets would there be on a diamond like that?" Robert Sandy asked.

"Fifty-eight."

"You mean you know exactly?"

"Yes, I know exactly."

"Good Lord. And what roughly would you say it is worth?"

"A diamond like this," Harry Gold said, taking it from the paper and placing it in his palm, "a D colour stone of this size and clarity would command on enquiry a trade price of between twenty-five and thirty thousand dollars a carat. In the shops it would cost you double that. Up to sixty thousand dollars a carat in the retail market."

"Great Scott!" Robert Sandy cried, jumping up. The little jeweller's words seemed to have lifted him clean out of his seat. He stood there, stunned.

"And now," Harry Gold was saying, "we must find out precisely how many carats it weighs." He crossed over to a shelf on which there stood a small metal apparatus. "This is simply an electronic scale," he said. He slid back a glass door and placed the diamond inside. He twiddled a couple of knobs, then he read off the figures on a dial. "It weighs fifteen point two seven carats," he said. "And that, in case it interests you, makes it worth about half a million dollars in the trade and over one million dollars if you bought it in a shop."

"You are making me nervous," Robert Sandy said, laughing nervously.

"If I owned it," Harry Gold said, "it would make *me* nervous. Sit down again so you don't faint."

Robert Sandy sat down.

Harry Gold took his time settling himself into his chair behind the big partner's desk. "This is quite an occasion, Mr Sandy," he said. "I don't often have the pleasure of giving someone quite such a startlingly wonderful shock as this. I think I'm enjoying it more than you are."

"I am too shocked to be really enjoying it yet," Robert Sandy said. "Give me a moment or two to recover."

"Mind you," Harry Gold said, "one wouldn't expect much less from the King of the Saudis. Did you save the young prince's life?"

"I suppose I did, yes."

"Then that explains it." Harry Gold had put the diamond back on to the fold of white paper on his desk, and he sat there looking at it with the eyes of a man who loved what he saw. "My guess is that this stone came from the treasure-chest of old King Ibn Saud of Arabia. If that is the case, then it will be totally unknown in the trade, which makes it even more desirable. Are you going to sell it?"

"Oh gosh, I don't know what I am going to do with it," Robert Sandy said. "It's all so sudden and confusing."

"May I give you some advice?"

"Please do."

"If you *are* going to sell it, you should take it to auction. An unseen stone like this would attract a lot of interest, and the wealthy private buyers would be sure to come in and bid against the trade. And if you were able to reveal its provenance as well, telling them that it came directly from the Saudi Royal Family, then the price would go through the roof."

"You have been more than kind to me," Robert Sandy said. "When I do decide to sell it, I shall come first of all to you for advice. But tell me, does a diamond really cost twice as much in the shops as it does in the trade?"

"I shouldn't be telling you this," Harry Gold said, "but I'm afraid it does."

"So if you buy one in Bond Street or anywhere else like that, you are actually paying twice its intrinsic worth?"

"That's more or less right. A lot of young ladies have received nasty shocks when they've tried to re-sell jewellery that has been given to them by gentlemen."

"So diamonds are not a girl's best friend?"

"They are still very friendly things to have," Harry Gold said, "as you have just found out. But they are not generally a good investment for the amateur."

*

Outside in The High, Robert Sandy mounted his bicycle and headed for home. He was feeling totally light-headed. It was as though he had just finished a whole bottle of good wine all by himself. Here he was, solid old Robert Sandy, sedate and sensible, cycling through the streets of Oxford with more than half a million dollars in the pocket of his old tweed jacket! It was madness. But it was true.

He arrived back at his house in Acacia Road at about half-past four and parked his bike in the garage alongside the car. Suddenly he found himself running along the little concrete path that led to the front door. "Now stop that!" he said aloud, pulling up short. "Calm down. You've got to make this really good for Betty. Unfold it slowly." But oh, he simply *could not wait* to give the news to his lovely wife and watch her face as he told her the whole story of his afternoon. He found her in the kitchen packing some jars of home-made jam into a basket.

"Robert!" she cried, delighted as always to see him. "You're home early! How nice!"

He kissed her and said, "I *am* a bit early, aren't I?"

"You haven't forgotten we're going to the Renshaws for the weekend? We have to leave fairly soon."

"I had forgotten," he said. "Or maybe I hadn't. Perhaps that's why I'm home early."

"I thought I'd take Margaret some jam."

"Good," he said. "Very good. You take her some jam. That's a very good idea to take Margaret some jam."

There was something in the way he was acting that made her swing round and stare at him. "Robert," she said, "what's happened? There's something the matter."

"Pour us each a drink," he said. "I've got a bit of news for you."

"Oh darling, it's not something awful, is it?"

"No," he said. "It's something funny. I think you'll like it."

"You've been made Head of Surgery!"

"It's funnier than that," he said. "Go on, make a good stiff drink for each of us and sit down and I'll tell you."

"It's a bit early for drinks," she said, but she got the ice-tray from the fridge and started making his whisky and soda. While she was doing this, she kept glancing up at him nervously. She said, "I don't think I've ever seen you quite like this before. You are wildly excited about something and you are pretending to be very calm. You're all red in the face. Are you sure it's good news?"

"I *think* it is," he said, "but I'll let you judge that for yourself." He sat down at the kitchen table and watched her as she put the glass of whisky in front of him.

"All right," she said. "Come on. Let's have it."

"Get a drink for yourself first," he said.

"My goodness, what is this?" she said, but she poured some gin into a glass and was reaching for the ice-tray when he said, "More than that. Give yourself a good stiff one."

"Now I *am* worried," she said, but she did as she was told and then added ice and filled the glass up with tonic. "Now then," she said, sitting down beside him at the table, "get it off your chest."

Robert began telling his story. He started with the Prince in the consulting-room and he spun it out long and well so that it took a good ten minutes before he came to the diamond.

"It must be quite a whopper," she said, "to make you go all red in the face and funny-looking."

He reached into his pocket and took out the little black pouch and put it on the table. "There it is," he said. "What do you think?"

She loosened the silk cord and tipped the stone into her hand. "Oh, my God!" she cried. "It's absolutely stunning!"

"It is, isn't it."

"It's amazing."

"I haven't told you the whole story yet," he said,

and while his wife rolled the diamond from the palm of one hand to the other, he went on to tell her about his visit to Harry Gold in The High. When he came to the point where the jeweller began to talk about value, he stopped and said, "So what do you think he said it was worth?"

"Something pretty big," she said. "It's bound to be. I mean just *look* at it!"

"Go on then, make a guess. How much?"

"Ten thousand pounds," she said. "I really don't have any idea."

"Try again."

"You mean, it's more?"

"Yes, it's quite a lot more."

"Twenty thousand pounds!"

"Would you be thrilled if it was worth as much as that?"

"Of course, I would, darling. Is it really worth twenty thousand pounds?"

"Yes," he said. "And the rest."

"Now don't be a beast, Robert. Just tell me what Mr Gold said."

"Take another drink of gin."

She did so, then put down the glass, looking at him and waiting.

"It is worth at least half a million dollars and very probably over a million."

"You're joking!" Her words came out in a kind of gasp.

"It's known as a pear-shape," he said. "And where it comes to a point at this end, it's as sharp as a needle."

"I'm completely stunned," she said, still gasping.

"You wouldn't have thought half a million, would you?"

"I've never in my life had to think in those sort of figures," she said. She stood up and went over to him and gave him a huge hug and a kiss. "You really are the most wonderful and stupendous man in the world!" she cried.

"I was totally bowled over," he said. "I still am."

"Oh, Robert!" she cried, gazing at him with eyes bright as two stars. "Do you realize what this means? It means we can get Diana and her husband out of that horrid little flat and buy them a small house!"

"By golly, you're right!"

"And we can buy a decent flat for John and give him a better allowance all the way through his medical school! And Ben . . . Ben wouldn't have to go on a motorbike to work all through the freezing winters. We could get him something better. And . . . and . . . and . . ."

"And what?" he asked, smiling at her.

"And you and I can take a really good holiday for

once and go wherever we please! We can go to Egypt and Turkey and you can visit Baalbek and all the other places you've been longing to go to for years and years!" She was quite breathless with the vista of small pleasures that were unfolding in her dreams. "And you can start collecting some really nice pieces for once in your life as well!"

Ever since he had been a student, Robert Sandy's passion had been the history of the Mediterranean countries, Italy, Greece, Turkey, Syria and Egypt, and he had made himself into something of an expert on the ancient world of those various civilizations. He had done it by reading and studying and by visiting, when he had the time, the British Museum and the Achmolean. But with three children to educate and with a job that paid only a reasonable salary, he had never been able to indulge this passion as he would have liked. He wanted above all to visit some of the grand remote regions of Asia Minor and also the now below-ground village of Babylon in Iraq and he would love to see the Arch of Ctsephon and the Spinx at Memphis and a hundred other things and places, but neither the time nor the money had ever been available. Even so, the long coffee-table in the living-room was covered with small objects and fragments that he had managed to pick up cheaply here and there through his life.

There was a mysterious pale alabaster *ushaptiu* in the form of a mummy from Upper Egypt which he knew was Pre-Dynastic from about 7000 BC. There was a bronze bowl from Lydia with an engraving on it of a horse, and an early Byzantine twisted silver necklace, and a section of a wooden painted mask from an Egyptian sarcophagus, and a Roman red-ware bowl, and a small black Etruscan dish, and perhaps fifty other fragile and interesting little pieces. None was particularly valuable, but Robert Sandy loved them all.

"Wouldn't that be marvellous?" his wife was saying. "Where shall we go first?"

"Turkey," he said.

"Listen," she said, pointing to the diamond that lay sparkling on the kitchen table, "you'd better put your fortune away somewhere safe before you lose it."

"Today is Friday," he said. "When do we get back from the Renshaws?"

"Sunday night."

"And what are we going to do with our million-pound rock in the meanwhile? Take it with us in my pocket?"

"No," she said, "that would be silly. You really cannot walk around with a million pounds in your pocket for a whole weekend. It's got to go into a safe-

79

deposit box at the bank. We should do it now."

"It's Friday night, my darling. All the banks are closed till next Monday."

"So they are," she said. "Well then, we'd better hide it somewhere in the house."

"The house will be empty till we come back," he said. "I don't think that's a very good idea."

"It's better than carrying it around in your pocket or in my handbag."

"I'm not leaving it in the house. An empty house is always liable to be burgled."

"Come on, darling," she said, "surely we can think of a place where no one could possibly find it."

"In the teapot," he said.

"Or bury it in the sugar-basin," she said.

"Or put it in the bowl of one of my pipes in the pipe-rack," he said. "With some tobacco over it."

"Or under the soil of the azalea plant," she said.

"Hey, that's not bad, Betty. That's the best so far."

They sat at the kitchen table with the shining stone lying there between them, wondering very seriously what to do with it for the next two days while they were away.

"I still think it's best if I take it with me," he said.

"I don't, Robert. You'll be feeling in your pocket every five minutes to make sure it's still there. You won't relax for one moment."

"I suppose you're right," he said. "Very well, then. *Shall* we bury it under the soil of the azalea plant in the sitting-room? No one's going to look there."

"It's not one hundred per cent safe," she said. "Someone could knock the pot over and the soil would spill out on the floor and presto, there's a sparkling diamond lying there."

"It's a thousand to one against that," he said. "It's a thousand to one against the house being broken into anyway."

"No, it's not," she said. "Houses are being burgled every day. It's not worth chancing it. But look, darling, I'm not going to let this thing become a nuisance to you, or a worry."

"I agree with that," he said.

They sipped their drinks for a while in silence.

"I've got it!" she cried, leaping up from her chair. "I've thought of a marvellous place!"

"Where?"

"In here," she cried, picking up the ice-tray and pointing to one of the empty compartments. "We'll just drop it in here and fill it with water and put it back in the freezer. In an hour or two it'll be hidden inside a solid block of ice and even if you looked, you wouldn't be able to see it."

Robert Sandy stared at the ice-tray. "It's fantastic!" he said. "You're a genius! Let's do it right away!"

"Shall we really do it?"

"Of course. It's a terrific idea."

She picked up the diamond and placed it into one of the little empty compartments. She went to the sink and carefully filled the whole tray with water. She opened the door of the freezer section of the fridge and slid the tray in. "It's the top tray on the left," she said. "We'd better remember that. And it'll be in the block of ice furthest away on the right hand side of the tray."

"The top tray on the left," he said. "Got it. I feel better now that it's tucked safely away."

"Finish your drink, darling," she said. "Then we must be off. I've packed your case for you. And we'll try not to think about our million pounds any more until we come back."

"Do we talk about it to other people?" he asked her. "Like the Renshaws or anyone else who might be there?"

"I wouldn't," she said. "It's such an incredible story that it would soon spread around all over the place. Next thing you know, it would be in the papers."

"I don't think the King of the Saudis would like that."

"Nor do I. So let's say nothing at the moment."

"I agree," he said. "I would hate any kind of publicity."

"You'll be able to get yourself a new car," she said, laughing.

"So I will. I'll get one for you too. What kind would you like, darling?"

"I'll think about it," she said.

Soon after that, the two of them drove off to the Renshaws for the weekend. It wasn't far, just beyond Whitney, some thirty minutes from their own house. Charlie Renshaw was a consultant physician at the hospital and the families had known each other for many years.

The weekend was pleasant and uneventful, and on Sunday evening Robert and Betty Sandy drove home again, arriving at the house in Acacia Road at about seven p.m. Robert took the two small suitcases from the car and they walked up the path together. He unlocked the front door and held it open for his wife.

"I'll make some scrambled eggs," she said, "and crispy bacon. Would you like a drink first, darling?"

"Why not?" he said.

He closed the door and was about to carry the suitcases upstairs when he heard a piercing scream from the sitting-room. "*Oh no!*" she was crying. "*No! No! No!*"

Robert dropped the suitcase and rushed in after her. She was standing there pressing her hands to her cheeks and already tears were streaming down her face.

The scene in the sitting-room was one of utter desolation. The curtains were drawn and they seemed to be the only things that remained intact in the room. Everything else had been smashed to smithereens. All Robert Sandy's precious little objects from the coffee-table had been picked up and flung against the walls and were lying in tiny pieces on the carpet. A glass cabinet had been tipped over. A chest-of-drawers had had its four drawers pulled out and the contents, photographs albums, games of Scrabble and Monopoly and a chessboard and chessmen and many other family things had been flung across the room. Every single book had been pulled out of the big floor-to-ceiling bookshelves against the far wall and piles of them were now lying open and mutilated all over the place. The glass on each of the four watercolours had been smashed and the oil painting of their three children painted when they were young had had its canvas slashed many times with a knife. The armchairs and the sofa had also been slashed so that the stuffing was bulging out. Virtually everything in the room except the curtains and the carpet had been destroyed.

"Oh, Robert," she said, collapsing into his arms, "I don't think I can stand this."

He didn't say anything. He felt physically sick.

"Stay here," he said. "I'm going to look upstairs." He ran out and took the stairs two at a time and went first to their bedroom. It was the same in there. The drawers had been pulled out and the shirts and blouses and underclothes were now scattered everywhere. The bedclothes had been stripped from the double bed and even the mattress had been tipped off the bed and slashed many times with a knife. The cupboards were open and every dress and suit and every pair of trousers and every jacket and every skirt had been ripped from its hanger. He didn't look in the other bedrooms. He ran downstairs and put an arm around his wife's shoulders and together they picked their way through the debris of the sitting-room towards the kitchen. There they stopped.

The mess in the kitchen was indescribable. Almost every single container of any sort in the entire room had been emptied on to the floor and then smashed to pieces. The place was a waste-land of broken jars and bottles and food of every kind. All Betty's home-made jams and pickles and bottled fruits had been swept from the long shelf and lay shattered on the ground. The same had happened to the stuff in the store-cupboard, the mayonnaise, the ketchup, the vinegar, the olive oil, the vegetable oil and all the rest. There were two other long shelves on the far wall and on these had stood about twenty lovely large glass jars with big ground-glass stoppers in which were kept rice and flour and brown sugar and bran and oatmeal and all sorts of other things. Every jar now lay on the floor in many pieces, with the contents spewed around. The refrigerator door was open and the things that had been inside, the leftover foods, the milk, the eggs, the butter, the yoghurt, the tomatoes, the lettuce, all of them had been pulled out and splashed on to the pretty tiled kitchen floor. The inner drawers of the fridge had been thrown into the mass of slush and trampled on. The plastic ice-trays had been yanked out and each had been literally broken in two and thrown aside. Even the plastic-coated shelves had been ripped out of the fridge and bent double and thrown down with the rest. All the bottles of drink, the whisky, gin, vodka, sherry, vermouth, as well as half a dozen cans of beer, were standing on the table, empty. The bottles of drink and the beer cans seemed to be the only things in the entire house that had not been smashed. Practically the whole floor lay under a thick layer of mush and goo. It was as if a gang of mad children had been told to see how much mess they could make and had succeeded brilliantly.

Robert and Betty Sandy stood on the edge of it all, speechless with horror. At last Robert said, "I imagine our lovely diamond is somewhere underneath all that."

"I don't give a damn about our diamond," Betty said. "I'd like to kill the people who did this."

"So would I," Robert said. "I've got to call the police." He went back into the sitting-room and picked up the telephone. By some miracle it still worked.

The first squad car arrived in a few minutes. It was followed over the next half-hour by a police inspector, a couple of plain-clothes men, a finger-print expert and a photographer.

The Inspector had a black moustache and a short muscular body. "These are not professional thieves," he told Robert Sandy after he had taken a look round. "They weren't even amateur thieves. They were simply hooligans off the street. Riff-raff. Yobbos. Probably three of them. People like this scout around looking for an empty house and when they find it they break in and the first thing they do is to hunt out the booze. Did you have much alcohol on the premises?"

"The usual stuff," Robert said. "Whisky, gin, vodka, sherry and a few cans of beer."

"They'll have drunk the lot," the Inspector said. "Lads like these have only two things in mind, drink and destruction. They collect all the booze on to a table and sit down and drink themselves raving mad. Then they go on the rampage."

"You mean they didn't come in here to steal?" Robert asked.

"I doubt they've stolen anything at all," the Inspector said. "If they'd been thieves they would at least have taken your TV set. Instead, they smashed it up."

"But why do they do this?"

"You'd better ask their parents," the Inspector said. "They're rubbish, that's all they are, just rubbish. People aren't brought up right any more these days."

Then Robert told the Inspector about the diamond. He gave him all the details from the beginning to end because he realized that from the police point of view it was likely to be the most important part of the whole business.

"Half a million quid!" cried the Inspector.

"Probably double that," Robert said.

"Then that's the first thing we look for," the Inspector said.

"I personally do not propose to go down on my hands and knees grubbing around in that pile of slush," Robert said. "I don't feel like it at this moment."

"Leave it to us," the Inspector said. "We'll find it. That was a clever place to hide it."

"My wife thought of it. But tell me, Inspector, if by some remote chance they *had* found it . . ."

"Impossible," the Inspector said. "How could they?"

"They might have seen it lying on the floor after the ice had melted," Robert said. "I agree it's unlikely. But if they *had* spotted it, would they have taken it?"

"I think they would," the Inspector said. "No one can resist a diamond. It has a sort of magnetism about it. Yes, if one of them had seen it on the floor,

I think he would have slipped it into his pocket. But don't worry about it, Doctor. It'll turn up."

"I'm not worrying about it," Robert said. "Right now, I'm worrying about my wife and about our house. My wife spent years trying to make this place into a good home."

"Now look, sir," the Inspector said, "the thing for you to do tonight is to take your wife off to a hotel and get some rest. Come back tomorrow, both of you, and we'll start sorting things out. There'll be someone here all the time looking after the house."

"I have to operate at the hospital first thing in the morning," Robert said. "But I expect my wife will try to come along."

"Good," the Inspector said. "It's a nasty upsetting business having your house ripped apart like this. It's a big shock. I've seen it many times. It hits you very hard."

Robert and Betty Sandy stayed the night at Oxford's Randolph Hotel, and by eight o'clock the following morning Robert was in the Operating Theatre at the hospital, beginning to work his way through his morning list.

Shortly after noon, Robert had finished his last operation, a straightforward non-malignant prostate on an elderly male. He removed his rubber gloves and mask and went next door to the surgeons' small rest-room for a cup of coffee. But before he got his coffee, he picked up the telephone and called his wife.

"How are you, darling?" he said.

"Oh, Robert, it's so *awful*," she said. "I just don't know where to begin."

"Have you called the insurance company?"

"Yes, they're coming any moment to help me make a list."

"Good," he said. "And have the police found our diamond?"

"I'm afraid not," she said. "They've been through every bit of that slush in the kitchen and they swear it's not there."

"Then where can it have gone? Do you think the vandals found it?"

"I suppose they must have," she said. "When they broke those ice-trays all the ice-cubes would have fallen out. They fall out when you just bend the tray. They're meant to."

"They still wouldn't have spotted it in the ice," Robert said.

"They would when the ice melted," she said. "Those men must have been in the house for hours. Plenty of time for it to melt."

"I suppose you're right."

"It would stick out a mile lying there on the floor,"

she said, "the way it shines."

"Oh dear," Robert said.

"If we never get it back we won't miss it much anyway, darling," she said. "We only had it a few hours."

"I agree," he said. "Do the police have any leads on who the vandals were?"

"Not a clue," she said. "They found lots of finger-prints, but they don't seem to belong to any known criminals."

"They wouldn't," he said, "not if they were hooligans off the street."

"That's what the Inspector said."

"Look, darling," he said, "I've just about finished here for the morning. I'm going to grab some coffee, then I'll come home to give you a hand."

"Good," she said. "I need you, Robert. I need you badly."

"Just give me five minutes to rest my feet," he said, "I feel exhausted."

In Number Two Operating Theatre not ten yards away, another senior surgeon called Brian Goff was also nearly finished for the morning. He was on his last patient, a young man who had a piece of bone lodged somewhere in his small intestine. Goff was being assisted by a rather jolly young Registrar named William Haddock, and between them they had opened the patient's abdomen and Goff was lifting out a section of the small intestine and feeling along it with his fingers. It was routine stuff and there was a good deal of conversation going on in the room.

"Did I ever tell you about the man who had lots of little live fish in his bladder?" William Haddock was saying.

"I don't think you did," Goff said.

"When we were students at Barts," William Haddock said, "we were being taught by a particularly unpleasant Professor of Urology. One day, this twit was going to demonstrate how to examine the bladder using a cystoscope. The patient was an old man suspected of having stones. Well now, in one of the hospital waiting-rooms, there was an aquarium that was full of those tiny little fish, neons they're called, brilliant colours, and one of the students sucked up about twenty of them into a syringe and managed to inject them into the patient's bladder when he was under his pre-med, before he was taken up to Theatre for his cystoscopy."

"That's disgusting!" the theatre sister cried. "You can stop right there, Mr Haddock!"

Brian Goff smiled behind his mask and said, "What

happened next?" As he spoke, he had about three feet of the patient's small intestine lying on the green sterile sheet, and he was still feeling along it with his fingers.

"When the Professor got the cystoscope into the bladder and put his eye to it," William Haddock said, "he started jumping up and down and shouting with excitement.

"'What is it, sir?' the guilty student asked him. 'What do you see?'

"'It's fish!' cried the Professor. 'There's hundreds of little fish! They're swimming about!'"

"You made it up," the theatre sister said. "It's not true."

"It most certainly is true," the Registrar said. "I looked down the cystoscope myself and saw the fish. And they were actually swimming about."

"We might have expected a fishy story from a man with a name like Haddock," Goff said. "Here we are," he added. "Here's this poor man's trouble. You want to feel it?"

William Haddock took the pale grey piece of intestine between his fingers and pressed. "Yes," he said. "Got it."

"And if you look just there," Goff said, instructing him, "you can see where the bit of bone has punctured the mucosa. It's already inflamed."

Brian Goff held the section of intestine in the palm of his left hand. The sister handed him a scalpel and he made a small incision. The sister gave him a pair of forceps and Goff probed down amongst all the slushy matter of the intestine until he found the offending object. He brought it out, held firmly in the forceps, and dropped it into the small stainless-steel bowl the sister was holding. The thing was covered in pale brown gunge.

"That's it," Goff said. "You can finish this one for me now, can't you, William. I was meant to be at a meeting downstairs fifteen minutes ago."

"You go ahead," William Haddock said. "I'll close him up."

The senior surgeon hurried out of the Theatre and the Registrar proceeded to sew up, first the incision in the intestine, then the abdomen itself. The whole thing took no more than a few minutes.

"I'm finished," he said to the anaesthetist.

The man nodded and removed the mask from the patient's face.

"Thank you, Sister," William Haddock said. "See you tomorrow." As he moved away, he picked up from the sister's tray the stainless-steel bowl that contained the gunge-covered brown object. "Ten to one it's a chicken bone," he said and he carried it to the sink and began rinsing it under the tap.

"Good God, what's this?" he cried. "Come and look, Sister!"

The sister came over to look. "It's a piece of costume jewellery," she said. "Probably part of a necklace. Now how on earth did he come to swallow that?"

"He'd have passed it if it hadn't had such a sharp point," William Haddock said. "I think I'll give it to my girlfriend."

"You can't do that, Mr Haddock," the sister said. "It belongs to the patient. Hang on a sec. Let me look at it again." She took the stone from William Haddock's gloved hand and carried it into the powerful light that hung over the operating table. The patient had now been lifted off the table and was being wheeled out into Recovery next door, accompanied by the anaesthetist.

"Come here, Mr Haddock," the sister said, and there was an edge of excitement in her voice. William Haddock joined her under the light. "This is amazing," she went on. "Just look at the way it sparkles and shines. A bit of glass wouldn't do that."

"Maybe it's rock-crystal," William Haddock said, "or topaz, one of those semi-precious stones."

"You know what I think," the sister said. "I think it's a diamond."

"Don't be silly," William Haddock said.

A junior nurse was wheeling away the instrument trolley and a male theatre assistant was helping to clear up. Neither of them took any notice of the young surgeon and the sister. The sister was about twenty-eight years old, and now that she had removed her mask she appeared as an extremely attractive young lady.

"It's easy enough to test it," William Haddock said. "See if it cuts glass."

Together they crossed over to the frosted-glass window of the operating-room. The sister held the stone between finger and thumb and pressed the sharp pointed end against the glass and drew it downward. There was a fierce scraping crunch as the point bit into the glass and left a deep line two inches long.

"Good grief!" William Haddock said. "It is a diamond!"

"If it is, it belongs to the patient," the sister said firmly.

"Maybe it does," William Haddock said, "but he was mighty glad to get rid of it. Hold on a moment. Where are his notes?" He hurried over to the side table and picked up a folder which said on it JOHN DIGGS. He opened the folder. In it there was an X-ray of the patient's intestine accompanied by the radiologist's report. *John Diggs*, the report said.

Age 17. Address 123 Mayfield Road, Oxford. There is clearly a large obstruction of some sort in the upper small intestine. The patient has no recollection of swallowing anything unusual, but says that he ate some fried chicken on Sunday evening. The object clearly has a sharp point that has pierced the mucosa of the intestine, and it could be a piece of bone . . .

"How could he swallow a thing like that without knowing it?" William Haddock said.

"It doesn't make sense," the sister said.

"There's no question it's a diamond after the way it cut the glass," William Haddock said. "Do you agree?"

"Absolutely," the sister said.

"And a big one at that," Haddock said. "The question is, how good a diamond is it? How much is it worth?"

"We'd better send it to the lab right away," the sister said.

"To heck with the lab," Haddock said. "Let's have a bit of fun and do it ourselves."

"How?"

"We'll take it to Golds, the jewellers in The High. They'll know. The thing must be worth a fortune. We're not going to steal it, but we're jolly well going to find out about it. Are you game?"

"Do you know anyone at Golds?" the sister said.

"No, but that doesn't matter. Do you have a car?"

"My Mini's in the car park."

"Right. Get changed. I'll meet you out there. It's about your lunch time anyway. I'll take the stone."

Twenty minutes later, at a quarter to one, the little Mini pulled up outside the jewellery shop of H. F. Gold and parked on the double-yellow lines. "Who cares," William Haddock said. "We won't be long." He and the sister went into the shop.

There were two customers inside, a young man and a girl. They were examining a tray of rings and were being served by the woman assistant. As soon as they came in, the assistant pressed a bell under the counter and Harry Gold emerged through the door at the back. "Yes," he said to William Haddock and the sister. "Can I help you?"

"Would you mind telling us what this is worth?" William Haddock said, placing the stone on a piece of green cloth that lay on the counter.

Harry Gold stopped dead. He stared at the stone. Then he looked up at the young man and woman who stood before him. He was thinking very fast. Steady now, he told himself. Don't do anything silly. Act natural.

"Well well," he said as casually as he could. "That looks to me like a very fine diamond, a very fine diamond indeed. Would you mind waiting a moment while I weigh it and examine it carefully in my office. Then perhaps I'll be able to give you an accurate valuation. Do sit down, both of you."

Harry Gold scuttled back into his office with the diamond in his hand. Immediately, he took it to the electronic scale and weighed it. Fifteen point two seven carats. That was exactly the weight of Mr Robert Sandy's stone! He had been certain it was the same one the moment he saw it. Who could mistake a diamond like that? And now the weight had proved it. His instinct was to call the police right away, but he was a cautious man who did not like making mistakes. Perhaps the doctor had already sold his diamond. Perhaps he had given it to his children. Who knows?

Quickly he picked up the Oxford telephone book. The Radcliffe Infirmary was Oxford 249891. He dialled it. He asked for Mr Robert Sandy. He got Robert's secretary. He told her it was most urgent that he speak to Mr Sandy this instant. The secretary said, "Hold on, please." She called the Operating Theatre. Mr Sandy had gone home half an hour ago, they told her. She took up the outside phone and relayed this information to Mr Gold.

"What's his home number?" Mr Gold asked her.

"Is this to do with a patient?"

"No!" cried Harry Gold. "It's to do with a robbery! For heaven's sake, woman, give me that number quickly!"

"Who is speaking, please?"

"Harry Gold! I'm the jeweller in The High! Don't waste time, I beg you!"

She gave him the number.

Harry Gold dialled again.

"Mr Sandy?"

"Speaking."

"This is Harry Gold, Mr Sandy, the jeweller. Have you by any chance lost your diamond?"

"Yes, I have."

"Two people have just brought it into my shop," Harry Gold whispered excitedly. "A man and a woman. Youngish. They're trying to get it valued. They're waiting out there now."

"Are you certain it's my stone?"

"Positive. I weighed it."

"Keep them there, Mr Gold!" Robert Sandy cried. "Talk to them! Humour them! Do anything! I'm calling the police!"

Robert Sandy called the police station. Within seconds, he was giving the news to the Detective Inspector who was in charge of the case. "Get there fast and you'll catch them both!" he said. "I'm on my way too!"

"Come on, darling!" he shouted to his wife. "Jump in the car. I think they've found our diamond and the thieves are in Harry Gold's shop right now trying to sell it!"

When Robert and Betty Sandy drove up to Harry Gold's shop nine minutes later, two police cars were already parked outside. "Come on, darling," Robert said. "Let's go in and see what's happening."

There was a good deal of activity inside the shop when Robert and Betty Sandy rushed in. Two policemen and two plain-clothes detectives, one of them the Inspector, were surrounding a furious William Haddock and an even more furious theatre sister. Both the young surgeon and the theatre sister were handcuffed.

"You found it *where*?" the Inspector was saying.

"Take these handcuffs off me!" the sister was shouting. "How dare you do this!"

"Tell us again where you found it," the Inspector said, caustic.

"In someone's stomach!" William Haddock yelled back at him. "I've told you twice!"

"Don't give me that!" the Inspector said.

"Good God, William!" Robert Sandy cried as he came in and saw who it was. "And Sister Wyman! What on earth are you two doing here?"

"They had the diamond," the Inspector said. "They

were trying to flog it. Do you know these people, Mr Sandy?"

It didn't take very long for William Haddock to explain to Robert Sandy, and indeed to the Inspector, exactly how and where the diamond had been found.

"Remove their handcuffs, for heaven's sake, Inspector," Robert Sandy said. "They're telling the truth. The man you want, at least one of the men you want, is in the hospital right now, just coming round from his anaesthetic. Isn't that right, William?"

"Correct," William Haddock said. "His name is John Diggs. He'll be in one of the surgical wards."

Harry Gold stepped forward. "Here's your diamond, Mr Sandy," he said.

"Now listen," the theatre sister said, still angry, "would someone for God's sake tell me how the patient came to swallow a diamond like this without knowing he'd done it?"

"I think I can guess," Robert Sandy said. "He allowed himself the luxury of putting ice in his drink. Then he got very drunk. Then he swallowed a piece of half-melted ice."

"I still don't get it," the sister said.

"I'll tell you the rest later," Robert Sandy said. "In fact, why don't we all go round the corner and have a drink ourselves?"

Spaghetti Pig-out

Paul Jennings

Guts Garvey was a real mean kid. He made my life miserable. I don't know why he didn't like me. I hadn't done anything to him. Not a thing.

He wouldn't let any of the other kids hang around with me. I was on my own. Anyone in the school who spoke to me was in his bad books. I wandered around the yard at lunch time like a dead leaf blown in the wind.

I tried everything. I even gave him my pocket money one week. He just bought a block of chocolate from the canteen and ate it in front of me. Without even giving me a bit. What a rat.

After school I only had one friend. My cat – Bad Smell. She was called that because now and then she would make a bad smell. Well, she couldn't help it. Everyone has their faults. She was a terrific cat. But still. A cat is not enough. You need other kids for friends too.

Even after school no one would come near me. I only had one thing to do. Watch the television. But that wasn't much good either. There were only little kids' shows on before tea.

"I wish we had a video," I said to Mum one night.

"We can't afford it, Matthew," said Mum. "Anyway, you watch too much television as it is. Why don't you go and do something with a friend?"

I didn't say anything. I couldn't tell her that I didn't have any friends. And never would have as long as Guts Garvey was around. A bit later Dad came in. He had a large parcel under his arm. "What have you got, Dad?" I asked.

"It's something good," he answered. He put the package on the lounge-room floor and I started to unwrap it. It was about the size of a large cake. It was green and spongy with an opening in the front.

"What is it?" I said.

"What you've always wanted. A video player."

I looked at it again. "I've never seen a video player like this before. It looks more like a mouldy loaf of bread with a hole in the front."

"Where did you get it?" asked Mum in a dangerous voice. "And how much was it?"

"I bought it off a bloke in the pub. A real bargain. Only fifty dollars."

"Fifty dollars is cheap for a video," I said. "But is

105

it a video? It doesn't look like one to me. Where are the cables?"

"He said it doesn't need cables. You just put in the video and press this." He handed me a green thing that looked like a bar of chocolate with a couple of liquorice blocks stuck on the top.

"You're joking," I said. "That's not a remote control."

"How much did you have to drink?" said Mum. "You must have been crazy to pay good money for that junk." She went off into the kitchen. I could tell that she was in a bad mood.

"Well at least try it," said Dad sadly. He handed me a video that he had hired down the street. It was called *Revenge of the Robots*. I pushed the video into the mushy hole and switched on the TV set. Nothing happened.

I looked at the liquorice blocks on the green chocolate thing. It was worth a try. I pushed one of the black squares.

The movie started playing at once. "It works," I yelled. "Good on you, Dad. It works. What a ripper."

Mum came in and smiled. "Well what do you know," she said. "Who would have thought that funny-looking thing was a video set? What will they think of next?"

*

Dad went out and helped Mum get tea while I sat down and watched the movie. I tried out all the liquorice-like buttons on the remote control. One was for fast forward, another was pause and another for rewind. The rewind was good. You could watch all the people doing things backwards.

I was rapt to have a video but to tell the truth the movie was a bit boring. I started to fiddle around with the handset. I pointed it at things in the room and pressed the buttons. I pretended that it was a ray gun.

"Tea time," said Mum after a while.

"What are we having?" I yelled.

"Spaghetti," said Mum.

I put the video on pause and went to the door. I was just about to say, "I'm not hungry," when I noticed something. Bad Smell was sitting staring at the TV in a funny way. I couldn't figure out what it was at first but I could see that something was wrong. She was so still. I had never seen a cat sit so still before. Her tail didn't swish. Her eyes didn't blink. She just sat there like a statue. I took off my shoe and threw it over near her. She didn't move. Not one bit. Not one whisker.

"Dad," I yelled. "Something is wrong with Bad Smell."

He came into the lounge and looked at the poor

cat. It sat there staring up at the screen with glassy eyes. Dad waved his hand in front of her face. Nothing. Not a blink. "She's dead," said Dad.

"Oh no," I cried. "Not Bad Smell. Not her. She can't be. My only friend." I picked her up. She stayed in the sitting-up position. I put her back on the floor. No change. She sat there stiffly. I felt for a pulse but I couldn't feel one. Her chest wasn't moving. She wasn't breathing.

"Something's not quite right," said Dad. "But I can't figure out what it is."

"She shouldn't be sitting up," I yelled. "Dead cats don't sit up. They fall over with their legs pointed up."

Dad picked up Bad Smell and felt all over her. "It's no good, Matthew," he said. "She's gone. We will bury her in the garden after tea." He patted me on the head and went into the kitchen.

Tears came into my eyes. I hugged Bad Smell to my chest. She wasn't stiff. Dead cats should be stiff. I remembered a dead cat that I once saw on the footpath. I had picked it up by the tail and it hadn't bent. It had been like picking up a saucepan by the handle.

Bad Smell felt soft. Like a toy doll. Not stiff and hard like the cat on the footpath.

Suddenly I had an idea. I don't know what gave it

to me. It just sort of popped into my head. I picked up the funny-looking remote control, pointed it at Bad Smell and pressed the FORWARD button. The cat blinked, stretched, and stood up. I pressed PAUSE again and she froze. A statue again. But this time she was standing up.

I couldn't believe it. I rubbed my eyes. The pause button was working on my cat. I pressed FORWARD a second time and off she went. Walking into the kitchen as if nothing had happened.

Dad's voice boomed out from the kitchen. "Look. Bad Smell is alive." He picked her up and examined her. "She must have been in a coma. Just as well we didn't bury her." Dad had a big smile on his face. He put Bad Smell down and shook his head. I went back to the lounge.

I hit one of the liquorice-like buttons. None of them had anything written on them but by now I knew what each of them did.

Or I thought I did.

The movie started up again. I watched it for a while until a blowfly started buzzing around and annoying me. I pointed the handset at it just for fun and pressed FAST FORWARD. The fly vanished. Or that's what seemed to happen. It was gone from sight but I could still hear it. The noise was tremendous. It was like a tiny jet fighter screaming around in the room. I saw something flash by. It whipped past me again. And again. And again. The blowfly was going so fast that I couldn't see it.

I pushed the PAUSE button and pointed it up where the noise was coming from. The fly must have gone right through the beam because it suddenly appeared out of nowhere. It hung silently in mid air. Still. Solidified. A floating, frozen fly. I pointed the handset at it again and pressed FORWARD. The blowfly came to life at once. It buzzed around the room at its normal speed.

"Come on," yelled Mum. "Your tea is ready."

I wasn't interested in tea. I wasn't interested in anything except this fantastic remote control. It seemed to be able to make animals and insects freeze or go fast forward. I looked through the kitchen door at Dad. He had already started eating. Long pieces of spaghetti dangled from his mouth. He was chewing and sucking at the same time.

Now don't get me wrong. I love Dad. I always have. He is a terrific bloke. But one thing that he used to do really bugged me. It was the way he ate spaghetti. He sort of made slurping noises and the meat sauces gathered around his lips as he sucked. It used to get on my nerves. I think that's why I did what I did. I know it's a weak excuse. I shivered. Then I pointed the control at him and hit the PAUSE button.

Dad stopped eating. He turned rock solid and just sat there with the fork halfway up to his lips. His mouth was wide open. His eyes stared. The spaghetti hung from his fork like worms of concrete. He didn't blink. He didn't move. He was as stiff as a tree trunk.

Mum looked at him and laughed. "Good one," she said. "You'd do anything for a laugh, Arthur."

Dad didn't move.

"OK," said Mum. "That's enough. You're setting a bad example for Matthew by fooling around with your food like that."

My frozen father never so much as moved an eyeball. Mum gave him a friendly push on the shoulder and he started to topple. Over he went. He looked just like a statue that had been pushed off its mount. Crash. He lay on the ground. His hand still halfway up to his mouth. The solid spaghetti hung in the same position. Only now it stretched out sideways pointing at his toes.

Mum gave a little scream and rushed over to him. Quick as a flash I pointed the remote control at him and pressed FORWARD. The spaghetti dangled downwards. Dad sat up and rubbed his head. "What happened?" he asked.

"You had a little turn," said Mum in a worried voice. "You had better go straight down to the hospital and have a check-up. I'll get the car. Matthew, you stay here and finish your tea. We won't be long."

I was going to tell them about the remote control but something made me stop. I had a thought. If I told them about it they would take it off me. It was the last I would see of it for sure. If I kept it to myself I could take it to school. I could show Guts Garvey my fantastic new find. He would have to make friends with me now that I had something as good as this. Every kid in the school would want to have a go.

Dad and Mum came home after about two hours.

Dad went straight to bed. The doctor had told him to have a few days' rest. He said Dad had been working too hard. I took the remote control to bed with me. I didn't use it until the next day.

It was Saturday and I slept in. I did my morning jobs and set out to find Guts Garvey. He usually hung around the shops on Saturday with his tough mates.

The shopping centre was crowded. As I went I looked in the shop windows. In a small cafe I noticed a man and a woman having lunch. They were sitting at a table close to the window. I could see everything that they were eating. The man was having a steak and what was left of a runny egg. He had almost finished his meal.

It reminded me of Dad and the spaghetti. I took out the remote control and looked at it. I knew that it could do PAUSE, FORWARD and FAST FORWARD. There was one more button. I couldn't remember what this last button was for. I pushed it.

I wouldn't have done it on purpose. I didn't really realize that it was pointing at the man in the shop. The poor thing.

The last button was REWIND.

Straight away he began to un-eat his meal. He went backwards. He put his fork up to his mouth and started taking out the food and placing it back on his plate. The runny egg came out of his mouth with bits of steak and chips. In, out, in, out, went his fork. Each time bringing a bit of food out of his mouth. He moved the mashed-up bits backwards on his plate with the knife and fork and they all formed up into solid chips, steak and eggs.

It was unbelievable. He was unchewing his food and un-eating his meal. Before I could gather my wits his whole meal was back on the plate. He then put his clean knife and fork down on the table.

My head swirled but suddenly I knew what I had to do. I pressed FORWARD. Straight away he picked up his knife and fork and began to eat his meal for the second time. The woman sitting opposite him had pushed her fist up into her mouth. She was terrified. She didn't know what was going on. Suddenly she screamed and ran out of the cafe. The man didn't take any notice, he just kept eating. He had to eat the whole meal again before he could stop.

I ran down the street feeling as guilty as sin. This thing was powerful. It could make people do things backwards.

I stopped at the corner. There, talking to his mean mate Rabbit, was Guts Garvey. This was my big chance to get into his good books. "Look," I said. "Take a squizz at this." I held out the remote control.

Guts Garvey grabbed it from my hand. "Yuck," he

growled. "Green chocolate. Buzz off, bird brain." He lifted the remote control. He was going to throw it at me.

"No," I yelled. "It's a remote control. From a video. You press the black things." Guts Garvey looked at me. Then he looked at the control. He didn't believe me but he pressed one of the buttons.

Rabbit was bouncing a basketball up and down on the footpath. He suddenly froze. So did the ball. Rabbit stood there on one leg and the ball floated without moving, halfway between his hand and the ground. Guts Garvey's mouth dropped open. He rubbed his eyes and looked again. The statue of Rabbit was still there.

"Press FORWARD," I said, pointing to the top button.

Guts pressed the control again and Rabbit finished bouncing the ball. I smiled. I could see that Guts was impressed. He turned and looked at me. Then he pointed the remote control straight at my face. "No," I screamed. "No."

But I was too late. Guts Garvey pressed the button. He "paused" me. I couldn't move. I just stood there with both arms frozen up in the air. My eyes stared. They didn't move. Nothing moved. I was rock solid. Guts and Rabbit laughed. Then they ran off.

*

People gathered round. At first they laughed. A whole circle of kids and adults looking at the stupid dill standing there like a statue. Someone waved their hand in front of my face. A girl poked me. "He's good," said someone. "He's not moving a muscle."

I tried to speak. My mouth wouldn't move. My tongue wouldn't budge. The crowd got bigger. I felt an idiot. What a fool. Dozens of people were staring at me wondering why I was standing there posed like a picture on the wall. Then I stopped feeling stupid. I felt scared. What if I stayed like this for ever? Not breathing. Not moving. Not alive, not dead. What would they do with me? Put me in the garden like a garden gnome? Stash me away in a museum? Bury me alive? It was too terrible to think about.

Suddenly I collapsed. I puddled on to the ground. Everyone laughed. I stood up and ran off as fast as I could go. As I ran I tried to figure it out. Why had I suddenly gone off pause? Then I realized what it was. I remembered my Uncle Frank's video. If you put it on pause and went away it would start up again automatically after three or four minutes. The movie would come off pause and keep going. That's what had happened to me.

I looked ahead. I could just make out two tiny figures in the distance. It was Rabbit and Guts Garvey. With my remote control. I had to get it back.

The dirty rats had nicked it. I didn't care about getting in Guts Garvey's good books any more. I just wanted my controller back.

And revenge. I wanted revenge.

I ran like a mad thing after them.

It was no good. I was out of breath and they were too far away. I couldn't catch them. I looked around. Shaun Potter, a kid from school, was sitting on his horse, Star, on the other side of the road. I rushed over to him. "Help," I said. "You've got to help. Guts Garvey has pinched my remote control. I've got to get it back. It's a matter of life and death."

Shaun looked at me. He wasn't a bad sort of kid. He was one of the few people in the school who had been kind to me. He wasn't exactly a friend. He was too scared of Guts Garvey for that. But I could tell by the way he smiled and nodded at me that he liked me. I jumped from foot to foot. I was beside myself. I had to get that remote control back. Shaun hesitated for a second or two. Then he said, "OK, hop up."

I put one foot in the stirrup and Shaun pulled me up behind him on to Star's back. "They went that way," I yelled.

Star went into a trot and then a canter. I held on for grim death. I had never been on a horse before. I bumped up and down behind Shaun. The ground seemed a long way down. I was scared but I didn't say anything. I had to catch Guts Garvey and Rabbit. We sped down the street past all the parked cars and people crossing the road.

"There they are," I yelled. Guts and Rabbit were in a line of people waiting for a bus. Shaun slowed Star down to a walk. Guts Garvey looked up and saw us. He pulled the remote control from his pocket. "Oh no," I yelled. "Not that."

I don't know whether or not Star sensed danger. Anyway, he did what horses often do at such times. He lifted up his tail and let a large steaming flow of horse droppings fall on to the road. Then he took a few steps towards Guts and the line of people.

Guts pointed the remote control at us and hit the REWIND button. "Stop," I screamed. But it was too late. Star began to go into reverse. She walked a few steps backwards. The pile of horse droppings began to stir. It twisted and lifted. Then it flew through the air – back to where it came from.

The line of people roared. Some laughed. Some screamed. Some ran off. How embarrassing. I was filled with shame. Poor Star went into a backwards trot. Then, suddenly she froze. We all froze. Guts had hit the PAUSE button. He had turned Shaun, Star and me into statues.

While we were standing there like stiff dummies

the bus pulled up. All the people in the queue piled on. They couldn't get on quickly enough. They wanted to get away from the mad boys and their even madder horse.

After four or five minutes the pause effect wore off. We were able to move. I climbed down off Star's back. "Sorry," I said to Shaun. "I didn't know this was going to happen."

Shaun stared down at me. He looked pale. "I think I've just had a bad dream," he said. "In the middle of the day. I think I'd better go home." He shook his head slowly and then trotted off.

"Rats," I said to myself. Everything was going wrong. I had lost the remote control. Guts Garvey had nicked it and there was nothing I could do about it. I was too scared to go near him in case he put me into reverse again. I felt terrible. I walked home with slow, sad footsteps.

When I got home Dad was mad because the remote control had disappeared. I couldn't tell him what had happened. He would never believe it. I had to spend most of the weekend pretending to help him look for it. The video wouldn't work without the control.

On Monday it was back to school as usual. Back to wandering around with no one to talk to.

As I walked around the schoolyard my stomach rumbled. I was hungry. Very hungry. I hadn't had anything to eat since tea time on Friday night. The reason for this was simple. This was the day of The Great Spaghetti Pig-Out. A competition to see who could eat the most spaghetti bolognese in fifteen minutes.

The grand final was to be held in the school hall. The winner received a free trip to Australia for two and the entrance money went to charity. I had a good chance of winning. Even though I was skinny I could eat a lot when I was hungry. I had won all the heats. My record was ten bowls of spaghetti bolognese in fifteen minutes. Maybe if I won the competition I would also win the respect of the kids. I was going to give the tickets to Australia to Mum and Dad. They needed a holiday badly.

I didn't see Guts Garvey until just before the competition. He kept out of my sight all day. I knew he was cooking up some scheme but I didn't know what it was.

There were four of us up on the platform. Me, two girls and Guts Garvey. The hall was packed with kids and teachers. I felt confident but nervous. I knew that I could win. I looked at Guts Garvey and saw that he was grinning his head off. Then I saw Rabbit in the front row. His pocket was bulging. Rabbit had something in his pocket and I thought I knew what it was.

They were up to no good. Guts and Rabbit had something cooked up and it wasn't spaghetti.

The plates of steaming spaghetti bolognese were lined up in front of us. Everything was ready for the starter to say "go". My empty stomach was in a knot. My mind was spinning. I tried to figure out what they were up to. What if I ate five plates of spaghetti and Rabbit put me into reverse? I would un-eat it like the man in the cafe. I would go backwards and take all of the spaghetti out and put it back on the plate. My knees started to knock.

I decided to back out of the competition. I couldn't go through with it.

"Go," yelled Mr Stepney, the school principal. It was too late. I had to go on.

I started shovelling spaghetti into my mouth. There was no time to mix in the meat sauce. I just pushed in the platefuls as they came. One, two, three. The winner would be the one to eat the most plates in fifteen minutes.

I watched Guts and the others out of the corner of my eye. I was already ahead by two bowls. In, out, in, out. Spaghetti, spaghetti, spaghetti. I was up to seven bowls, Guts had eaten only four and the two girls had managed two each. I was going to win.

Mum and Dad would be pleased.

Rabbit was watching us from the front row. I noticed Guts nod to him. Rabbit took something out of his pocket. I could see that it was the remote control. He was going to put me on rewind. I was gone.

But no. Rabbit was not pointing the control at me. He pointed it at Guts. What was going on? I soon found out. Guts began eating the spaghetti at enormous speed. Just like a movie on fast forward. His fork went up and down to his mouth so quickly that you could hardly see it. He licked like lightning. He swallowed at top speed. Boy did he go. His arms whirled. The spaghetti flew. Ten, eleven, twelve bowls. Thirteen, fourteen, fifteen. He was plates ahead. I didn't have a chance to catch up to Guts the guzzling gourmet. He fed his face like a whirlwind. It was incredible. Inedible. But it really happened.

Rabbit had put Guts on FAST FORWARD so that he would eat more plates than me in the fifteen minutes. It wasn't fair. But there was nothing I could do.

The audience cheered and shouted. They thought that Guts was fantastic. No one had ever seen anything like it before. He was up to forty bowls. I had only eaten ten and the two girls six each. The siren blew. Guts was the winner. I was second.

He had eaten forty bowls. No one had ever eaten

forty bowls of spaghetti before. Rabbit hit FORWARD on the control and Guts stopped eating. Everyone cheered Guts. I looked at my shoes. I felt ill and it wasn't just from eating ten plates of spaghetti. I swallowed. I had to keep it all down. That was one of the rules – you weren't allowed to be sick. If you threw up you lost the competition.

Guts stood up. He looked a bit funny. His face was a green colour. His stomach swelled out over his belt. He started to sway from side to side. Then he opened his mouth.

Out it came. A great tumbling, surge of spew. A tidal wave of swallowed spaghetti and meat sauce. It flowed down the table and on to the floor. A brown and white lake of sick. Guts staggered and tottered. He lurched to the edge of the stage. He opened his mouth again and let forth another avalanche. The kids in the front row screamed as the putrid waterfall splashed down. All over Rabbit.

Rabbit shrieked and sent the remote control spinning into the air. I jumped forward and grabbed it.

I shouldn't have done what I did. But I couldn't help myself. I pointed the control at Guts and the river of sick.

Then I pressed REWIND.

After that Guts Garvey was not very popular at school. To say the least. But I had lots of friends. And Mum and Dad had a great time in Australia.

And as to what happened to the remote control . . . Well. That's another story.

The Werewolf Mask

Kenneth Ireland

The mask looked just like a horrible werewolf with blood dripping from its fangs. It was one which fitted right over Peter's head, with spaces for his eyes so that when he looked out the movement gave an extra dimension of horror to the already terrifying expression on the rubber face. The hair hanging down from the top of the mask looked real, as did the hair and whiskers drooping from the sides and face. It was very satisfying, Peter felt, as soon as he had been in the joke shop and bought it.

Something, however, was missing. While the mask seemed realistic enough, it was his hands which were wrong. If a human could really turn into a werewolf, it would not be only the face which would change, but the hands would grow hairy as well. He discovered this when he unwrapped the paper bag in which he had bought it and went upstairs to try the effect in front of his dressing-table mirror. As long as

125

he kept his hands hidden, all was well, but once his hands were seen, they were far too smooth. In fact, they weren't hairy at all. It was rather disappointing, but nevertheless he thought that he'd try out the effect anyway. His mother was in, so making grunting and drooling noises he loped away down the stairs.

He went into the living-room where his mother was darning some socks, flung open the door suddenly and leaped in, arms raised to his shoulders, fingers extended like claws, and growling fiercely.

"My goodness," said his mother, looking up, "what on earth made you waste your money on a thing like that?"

"I thought it was rather good," said Peter, not at all put out. "Doesn't it look – well, real?"

"Well, it was your birthday money, so I suppose you could spend it how you liked," said his mother placidly, returning to the socks. "I don't know how you manage to get such large holes in these, I really don't. I think it must be the way you drag them on."

"But doesn't it look just like a werewolf?" asked Peter, taking the mask off and examining it carefully.

"It would, I suppose, except there are no such things and never have been such things as werewolves. I think you've wasted your money on something which is of no real use," his mother replied. "The money would have been better spent on some new pairs of socks. Still, your Aunty Doreen did tell you to spend it on something to amuse you, so I suppose we can't expect everything."

"The thing that's wrong with it is my hands," said Peter. "The face is all right, but the hands are wrong to go with it, don't you think?"

He put the mask on again and held his hands out for her to see the effect. She glanced at him briefly. "Putting a mask on like that won't make your hands look different from a boy's," she said. "The only thing you could do is wear gloves, your woolly ones perhaps, to disguise them."

Since she was taking no more notice of him, he went back upstairs, drew a pair of woolly gloves from a drawer in his dressing table, and tried the effect this time. Well, perhaps it wasn't all that bad. At least the gloves gave some kind of appearance of hairiness, but it was still not quite right. He tried combing the backs of the gloves, but that was no good at all. When he tried the claw effect, it was not half as good as when his nails were showing.

He still had some money left, so he went back to the joke shop, taking the mask with him.

"Have you got," he asked, "anything like hairy hands?"

The shopkeeper, being a bit of a joker himself,

looked down at his hands and asked if they would do. Then he looked down at his feet behind the counter and as if in surprise announced that he hadn't got pigs' trotters, either.

"No, I mean," explained Peter carefully, "like I bought this werewolf mask, I wonder if you have a kind of hairy hand mask to go with it. You know, to make the whole thing look – well, more real?"

"Hairy, with sort of claws, you mean?" asked the shopkeeper, nodding. "I might have. Hang on."

He went along the shelves behind the counter, opened first one drawer then another, and at the third drawer extracted a transparent plastic bag which he placed on the counter.

"These do?" he asked.

Peter picked them up eagerly, and inspected the contents through the plastic. They looked about right.

"Can I try them on?" he asked.

"Sure." The shopkeeper ripped open the bag and laid the hands out for him.

They were not like gloves, because they did not cover the hands all round, but merely lay on top and were fastened by a strap underneath and another round the wrist. Just the tips of the fingers fitted into sockets so that the rubber fingers would not dangle about uselessly. Peter tried them on.

"You can't expect a perfect fit," the shopkeeper said, "because of course they don't make them in different sizes. If they're too big, just tighten the strap underneath and pull the one that goes round your wrist up your arm a bit."

He helped him to put them on. They were rather big, but with them pulled well up the hands and over his wrists they were not bad at all, Peter decided. He would have them, if he could afford them. They were just as good as the magnificent mask, they had what looked like real hair growing along the backs, really satisfying long claws with just enough red on the ends to look as if they had torn into somebody's flesh, and what was more the red was actually painted to look as if it were still wet.

"Try the effect of both the mask and the hands," suggested the shopkeeper, pointing toward a mirror on the wall behind the door, so Peter did. That was much better, especially in the fairly dim light inside the shop. Absolutely terrifying, almost.

"Wrap them up for you?" asked the shopkeeper.

"No, I'll take them as they are," said Peter.

"Pardon?" The mask was not adjusted quite correctly, so his voice had been rather muffled.

Peter straightened the mask round his face so that his mouth was in the right place. "No thanks. How much?"

He paid the money and left the shop wearing his new possessions, because he just happened to have noticed Billy Fidler leaning against the pillar box outside, looking the other way.

He ran out of the shop, crept round the side of the pillar box then slowly reached out a hand to touch Billy on the shoulder. Billy turned, as he expected him to do.

"That's pretty good," said Billy, standing up. He looked Peter over critically. "I like the hands." Then he peered closer. "Oh – it's Peter."

"What do you think of it, then?" asked Peter.

"Pretty good. I could only really tell who you were by the clothes. It needs to be darker, though. I mean, you don't expect to come across a werewolf in daylight, so it looks just like a horrible mask and a pair of hands just now. If it was dark, though, and you suddenly came at me, that would really give me a nasty turn, I can tell you. Can I try them on?"

Peter didn't mind showing off his new acquisitions, and in any case he wanted to find out if what Billy had said was true. When Billy put them on, he found that it was. They were very good indeed, very effective for what they were, money well spent. But it was still unfortunately true that in broad daylight, on the pavement outside a row of shops with a pillar box just next to them, the mask was just a mask, and the hands were obviously artificial: not at all bad, though.

"Try them out on her," advised Peter, seeing Wendy Glover approaching with her mother. She was a girl at their school who always seemed to frighten quite easily.

Billy obediently popped behind the pillar box, and as Wendy and her mother drew level suddenly jumped out in front of them. Wendy's mother drew her daughter a little closer to her with disdain.

"Billy Fidler, I should think," remarked Wendy primly to her mother as they continued along the pavement. She turned after they had walked a few

paces. "A bit silly, I think," she said loudly.

"I tell you, it'd be a different story if it was dark," said Billy firmly, taking the mask and the hands off again and giving them back to Peter. "You try it, and see if I'm not right."

Peter slipped the items into his pockets and went home, taking them upstairs and placing them carefully in the drawer of his dressing-table, trying not to fold them and cause creases to develop in them.

It began to grow dark quite early that evening, so at the first opportunity Peter slipped off upstairs, stood in front of the mirror and tried the mask on again without switching on his bedroom light. In the dusk, it looked beautifully eerie. When he strapped the werewolf hands on to his own and then tried the effect in full, he almost managed to frighten himself, it looked so real – that figure ready to leap out at him from the mirror.

Then he knew what was lacking, and ran downstairs into the kitchen, hurrying back up to his bedroom with a little pocket torch in his hands. This time he drew the curtains as well, and when the room was pitch black held the torch just underneath his chin and switched it on suddenly.

This time he really did jump in fright. In front of him was a monster, really horrible, writhing and drooling with just a hint of blood on the tips of its fangs and from its claws more blood shining in the light as if freshly drawn from a victim. He moved his left hand across his mouth as though trying to wipe it clean, and it was so realistic that he was glad to know that downstairs both of his parents were in the house.

"Well, well," he said aloud, very pleased now, and hurried to switch on the electric light.

He put out the torch, sat on his bed and watched himself in the mirror as he removed first the hands and then the mask. It was almost a relief to be able to see him return to his normal self again. The only thing was, when would he ever have the opportunity to try these things out properly?

His father was calling from downstairs. "Peter!"

"What?"

"Would you like to do something for me?"

"What?"

"Come down, and I'll tell you."

Peter was about to replace his toys in the drawer again, thought better of it and stuffed them into his pockets instead, with the torch. If his father wanted him to go out, this might be just the opportunity he had been wondering about. He went downstairs, to find his father waiting for him in the hall.

"I've just remembered a couple of errands I'd like

doing. You know the envelopes I've been putting through people's doors, collecting for the children's homes?"

"Yes." Good, his father did want him to go out, then.

"There are two houses I called to collect them from last night, but the occupants were out. Just those two. Would you mind popping round to see if they're in tonight and collect them for me if they are? Take this with you." He handed over a little card of identity which stated that Peter's father was an authorized collector for the children's homes. "Explain who you are. They'll know you anyway, I expect, but take it just in case."

"Which houses are they?"

"Number eighteen, along our road, Mr and Mrs Hubbard, then number forty-seven Devonshire Road. He's new, so I don't know his name."

"No trouble," said Peter. "Won't take me ten minutes, if that."

"OK, then. Remember, it's the children's homes envelopes you're asking for," his father called after him.

"I know," said Peter, hurrying.

Once he was clear of the house he carefully drew out of his pockets the mask, and put it on, then the hands, then with the little torch held ready he set off down the street.

Number eighteen was not far away, but as he walked towards it Peter realized that there was nobody out on the street but himself. It was nicely dark by now, and the sky was clouded over, but all at once a cloud slid to one side and he saw that somewhere up there was not only the moon but a full one at that. Just the right sort of night for a werewolf to be abroad, he was thinking as the cloud glided back into place again, so he adjusted the mask so that the eyes and the mouth were in the right places, and pulled up the hairy hands as far as they would go. Then he continued briskly towards number eighteen, where he knocked on the door, pocket torch at the ready.

For a while there was no answer, then he heard the chain behind the door rattle, then a pause.

"Who is it?" he heard a woman's voice ask from inside.

"I've come for the envelope for the children's homes," he said loudly.

"Just a minute."

There was another pause, and he assumed that Mrs Hubbard was trying to find the envelopes so that she could put ten pence inside it before opening the door. He got ready. Then the chain rattled a second time, and the door opened. As the figure of

Mrs Hubbard appeared, he switched on the torch, directly under his chin.

Mrs Hubbard started and stepped back. Peter stood motionless with the light unwavering underneath his chin. There was a gasp, Mrs Hubbard clutched at her chest, then the door slammed shut and he heard the chain rattle again and then a bolt clunk into place.

That was very good, Peter was thinking. He did think of knocking on the door again, this time with his mask off, but thought better of it. She might not come to the door twice. So now for whoever it was who lived at number forty-seven Devonshire Road.

This was a large, gloomy house, with some kind of tall fir trees growing in the front garden behind a thick hedge. He did not remember ever having visited this house before. He opened the wooden gate and walked up the path, to find the front door was not at the front of the house but at the side, with more thick hedge growing in front of it on the opposite side of the narrow path. He wondered how anyone ever managed to carry furniture into the house when the path was as narrow as that.

He did not need to flash his torch to find the bell, because it was one of those illuminated ones, with a name on a card underneath it. *Luke Anthrope*, it said. So that was the name of the man who lived there, he thought; what an unusual name. He pressed the bell, and at once could hear an angry buzzing from somewhere inside, not like a bell at all. Feeling secure and safe behind his mask, when there was no answer he pressed the button again, and this time he heard a man's voice from inside the hall of this dark house. That rather surprised him, since there were no lights switched on that he could see.

"Go round the back," it said hoarsely.

He walked further along the path to find a tall wooden gate, which opened easily, so he passed through it to see the back door of the house, and knocked on it. The door opened just as the moon came out again, but he was ready for it and had the torch under his chin immediately. Mr Anthrope did not frighten easily, however. He was a short man, with a thick beard and moustache, and he just stood there regarding Peter steadily.

"I've come for the envelope for the children's homes," explained Peter, switching his torch off since it was obviously having no effect.

"Ah yes," said Mr Anthrope, but made no move to go and fetch it.

"I've got a card here," said Peter, fumbling in his pocket with some difficulty since the hand masks rather got in the way. "It's my father's really, but it proves that you can give the envelope to me."

The short man continued to regard him without moving. "Switch that torch on again," he said, so Peter did.

"Do you know why you never see two robins on a Christmas card?" the man asked him suddenly.

Peter did not.

"It's because if you ever find two robins together, they fight each other to the death. Did you know that? You can only ever find one robin in one place at a time. The same with one or two other creatures."

Peter had no idea of what this Mr Anthrope was getting at. He had made no mention of robins. Robins had nothing to do with it. And what other creatures?

The man's face was beginning to change rather strangely in the moonlight, which was now shining full upon him. It was as if his beard was growing more straggly, somehow, and the face becoming more lined, and his lips seemed somehow to be thinner and more drawn back over his teeth. Peter only just noticed too, now that the light was brighter, how hairy this man's hands were. Peter turned off the torch, because he did not need it now.

Then Mr Anthrope did a very strange thing. He came right out to the edge of his doorstep and leaned forward towards Peter as if he was going to whisper something to him.

Then Mr Anthrope's mouth was somewhere near

his ear, and Peter, always curious, strained to be able to hear what Mr Anthrope was about to whisper to him. He was astonished then to feel the bones in the side of his neck crunching, and blood running down inside his shirt. He didn't even have time to cry out before long nails were tearing at his flesh.

Harriet's Horrible Dream

Anthony Horowitz

What made the dream so horrible was that it was so *vivid*. Harriet actually felt that she was sitting in a cinema, rather than lying in bed, watching a film about herself. And although she had once read that people only ever dream in black-and-white, her dream was in full Technicolor. She could see herself wearing her favourite pink dress and there were red bows in her hair. Not, of course, that Harriet would have *dreamed* of having a black and white dream. Only the best was good enough for her.

Nonetheless, this was one dream that she wished she wasn't having. Even as she lay there with her legs curled up and her arms tight against her sides, she wished that she could wake up and call for Fifi – her French nanny – to go and make the breakfast. This dream, which could have gone on for seconds but at the same time seemed to have stretched through the whole night, was a particularly horrid one. In fact it was more of a nightmare. That was the truth.

It began so beautifully. There was Harriet in her pink dress, skipping up the path of their lovely house just outside Bath, in Wiltshire. She could actually hear herself singing. She was on her way back from school, and a particularly good day it had been too. She had come top in spelling and even though she knew she had cheated – peeking at the words which she had hidden in her pencil case – she had still enjoyed going to the front of the class to receive her merit mark. Naturally, Jane Wilson (who had come second) had said some nasty things but Harriet had got her own back, "accidentally" spilling a glass of milk over the other girl during lunch.

She was glad to be home. Harriet's house was a huge, white building – nobody in the school had a bigger house than her – set in a perfect garden complete with its own stream and miniature waterfall. Her brand-new bicycle was leaning against the wall outside the front door although perhaps she should have put it in the garage as it had been left out in the rain for a week now and had already begun to rust. Well, that was Fifi's fault. If the nanny had put it away for her, it would be all right now. Harriet thought about complaining to her mother. She had a special face for when things went wrong and a way of

141

squeezing out buckets of tears. If she complained hard enough, perhaps Mummy would sack Fifi. That would be fun. Harriet had already managed to get four nannies sacked. The last one had only been there three weeks!

She opened the front door and it was then that things began to go wrong. Somehow she knew it even before she realized what was happening. But of course that was something that was often the case in dreams. Events happened so quickly that you were aware of them before they actually arrived.

Her father was home from work early. Harriet had already seen his Porsche parked in the drive. Guy Hubbard ran an antiques shop in Bath although he had recently started dabbling in other businesses too. There was a property he was developing in Bristol, and something to do with time-share apartments in Majorca. But antiques were his main love. He would tour the country visiting houses, often where people had recently died. He would introduce himself to the widows and take a look around, picking out the treasures with a practised eye. "That's a nice table," he would say. "I could give you fifty pounds for that. Cash in hand. No questions asked. What do you say?" And later on that same table would turn up in his shop with a price tag for five hundred or even five thousand pounds. This was the secret of Guy's success. The people he dealt with never had any idea how much their property was worth. But he did. He once said he could smell a valuable piece even before he saw it.

Right now he was in the front living-room, talking to his wife in a low, unhappy voice. Something had gone wrong. Terribly wrong. Harriet went over to the door and put her ear against the wood.

"We're finished," Guy was saying. "Done for. We've gone belly-up, my love. And there's nothing we can do."

"Have you lost it all?" his wife was saying. Hilda Hubbard had once been a hairdresser but it had been years since she had worked. Even so, she was always complaining that she was tired and took at least six holidays a year.

"The whole lot. It's this development. Jack and Barry have cleared out. Skipped the country. They've taken all the money and they've left me with all the debts."

"But what are we going to do?"

"Sell up and start again, old girl. We can do it. But the house is going to have to go. And the cars . . ."

"What about Harriet?"

"She'll have to move out of that fancy school for a start. It's going to be a state school from now on. And that cruise the two of you were going on. You're going to have to forget about that!"

Harriet had heard enough. She pushed open the door and marched into the room. Already her cheeks had gone bright red and she had pressed her lips together so tightly that they were pushing out, kissing the air.

"What's happened?" she exclaimed in a shrill voice. "What are you saying, Daddy? Why can't I go on the cruise?"

Guy looked at his daughter unhappily. "Were you listening outside?" he demanded.

Hilda was sitting in a chair, holding a glass of whisky. "Don't bully her, Guy," she said.

"Tell me! Tell me! Tell me!" Harriet had drawn herself up as if she was about to burst into tears. But she had already decided she wasn't going to cry. On the other hand, she might try one of her ear-splitting screams.

Guy Hubbard was standing beside the fireplace. He was a short man with black, slicked back hair and a small moustache. He was wearing a checked suit with a red handkerchief poking out of the top pocket. He and Harriet had never really been close. In fact, Harriet spoke to him as little as possible and usually only to ask him for money.

"You might as well know," he said. "I've just gone bankrupt."

"What?" Harriet felt the tears pricking her eyes despite herself.

"Don't be upset, my precious baby doll—" Hilda began.

"*Do* be upset!" Guy interrupted. "There are going to be a few changes around here, my girl. I can tell you that. You can forget your fancy clothes and your French nannies . . ."

"Fifi?"

"I fired her this morning."

"But I liked her!" The tears began to roll down Harriet's cheeks.

"You're going to have to start pulling your weight. By the time I've paid off all the debts we won't have enough money to pay for a tin of beans. You'll have to get a job. How old are you now? Fourteen?"

"I'm twelve!"

"Well, you can still get a paper round or something. And Hilda, you're going to have to go back to hair. Cut and blow dry at thirty quid a time." Guy took out a cigarette and lit it, blowing blue smoke into the air. "We'll buy a house in Bletchley or somewhere. One bedroom is all we can afford."

"So where will I sleep?" Harriet quavered.

"You can sleep in the bath."

And that was what did it. The tears were pouring now – not just out of Harriet's eyes but also, more revoltingly, out of her nose. At the same time she let out one of her loudest, shrillest screams. "I won't! I won't! I won't!" she yelled. "I'm not leaving this house and I'm not sleeping in the bath. This is all your fault, Daddy. I hate you and I've always hated you and I hate Mummy too and I am going on my cruise and if you stop me I'll report you to the NSPCC and the police and I'll tell everyone that you steal things from old ladies and you never pay any tax and you'll go to prison and see if I care!"

Harriet was screaming so loudly that she had

almost suffocated herself. She stopped and sucked in a great breath of air, then turned on her heel and flounced out of the room, slamming the door behind her. Even as she went, she heard her father mutter, "We're going to have to do something about that girl."

But then she was gone.

And then, as is so often the way in dreams, it was the next day, or perhaps the day after, and she was sitting at the breakfast table with her mother who was eating a bowl of low-fat muesli and reading the *Sun* when her father came into the kitchen.

"Good morning," he said.

Harriet ignored him.

"All right," Guy said. "I've listened to what you had to say and I've talked things over with your mother and it does seem that we're going to have to come to a new arrangement."

Harriet helped herself to a third crumpet and smothered it in butter. She was being very prim and lady-like, she thought. Very grown up. The effect was only spoiled when melted butter dribbled down her chin.

"We're moving," Guy went on. "But you're right. There isn't going to be room for you in the new set-up. You're too much of a little miss."

"Guy . . ." Hilda muttered, disapprovingly.

Her husband ignored her. "I've spoken to your Uncle Algernon," he said. "He's agreed to take you."

"I don't have an Uncle Algernon," Harriet sniffed.

"He's not really your uncle. But he's an old friend of the family. He runs a restaurant in London. The Sawney Bean. That's what it's called."

"That's a stupid name for a restaurant," Harriet said.

"Stupid or not, it's made a bomb. He's raking it in. And he needs a young girl like you. Don't ask me what for! Anyway, I've telephoned him today and he's driving down to pick you up. You can go with him. And maybe one day when we've sorted ourselves out . . ."

"I'll miss my little Harry-Warry!" Hilda moaned.

"You won't miss her at all! You've been too busy playing bridge and having your toes pedicured to look after her properly. Maybe that's why she's turned into such a spoilt little so-and-so. But it's too late now. He'll be here soon. You'd better go and pack a bag."

"My baby!" This time it was Hilda who began to cry, her tears dripping into her muesli.

"I'll take two bags," Harriet said. "And you'd better give me some pocket money too. Six months in advance!"

Uncle Algernon turned up at midday. After what

her father had said, Harriet had expected him to drive a Rolls-Royce or at the very least a Jaguar and was disappointed by her first sight of him, rattling up the drive in a rather battered white van with the restaurant name, SAWNEY BEAN, written in blood-red letters on the side.

The van stopped and a figure got out, almost impossibly, from the front seat. He was so tall that Harriet was unsure how he had ever managed to fit inside. As he straightened up, he was much taller than the van itself, his bald head higher even than the aerial on the roof. He was also revoltingly thin. It was as if a normal human being had been put on a rack and stretched. His legs and his arms, hanging loose by his side, seemed to be made of elastic. His face was unusually repulsive. Although he had no hair on his head, he had big, bushy eyebrows, which didn't quite fit over his small, glistening eyes. His skin was the colour of a ping-pong ball. His whole head was roughly the same shape. He was wearing a black coat with a fur collar round his neck and gleaming black shoes which squeaked when he walked.

Guy Hubbard was the first one out to greet him. "Hello, Archie!" he exclaimed. The two men shook hands. "How's business?"

"Busy. Very busy." Algernon had a soft, low voice

that reminded Harriet of an undertaker. "I can't hang around, Guy. I have to be back in town by lunch. Lunch!" He licked his lips with a wet, pink tongue. "Fully booked today. And tomorrow. And all week. Sawney Bean has been more successful than I would ever have imagined."

"Coining it in, I bet."

"You could say that."

"So have you got it, then?"

Algernon smiled and reached into the pocket of his coat, pulling out a crumpled brown envelope which he handed to Guy. Harriet watched, puzzled, from the front door. She knew what brown envelopes meant when her father was concerned. This man, Algernon, was obviously giving him money – and lots of it from the size of the envelope. But he was the one who was taking her away to look after her. So shouldn't Guy have been paying *him*?

Guy pocketed the money.

"So where is she?" Algernon asked.

"Harriet!" Guy called.

Harriet picked up her two suitcases and stepped out of the house for the last time. "I'm here," she said. "But I hope you're not expecting me to travel in that perfectly horrid little van . . ."

Guy scowled. But it seemed that Algernon hadn't heard her. He was staring at her with something in his eyes that was hard to define. He was certainly pleased by what he saw. He was happy. But there was something else. Hunger? Harriet could almost feel the eyes running up and down her body.

She put the cases down and grimaced as he ran a finger along the side of her face. "Oh yes," he breathed. "She's perfect. First class. She'll do very well."

"What will I do very well?" Harriet demanded.

"None of your business," Guy replied.

Meanwhile, Hilda had come out on to the drive. She was trembling and, Harriet noticed, refused to look at the new arrival.

"It's time to go," Guy said.

Algernon smiled at Harriet. He had dreadful teeth. They were yellow and uneven and – worse – strangely pointy. They were more like the teeth of an animal. "Get in," he said. "It's a long drive."

Hilda broke out in fresh tears. "Aren't you going to kiss me goodbye?" she wailed.

"No," Harriet replied.

"Goodbye," Guy said. He wanted to get this over with as soon as possible.

Harriet climbed into the van while Algernon placed her cases in the back. The front seat was covered in cheap plastic and it was torn in places, the stuffing oozing through. There was also a mess on the floor; sweet wrappers, old invoices and an empty cigarette pack. She tried to lower the window but the handle wouldn't turn.

"Goodbye, Mummy! Goodbye, Dad!" she called through the glass. "I never liked it here and I'm not sorry I'm going. Maybe I'll see you again when I'm grown up."

"I doubt it . . ." Had her father really said that? That was certainly what it sounded like. Harriet turned her head away in contempt.

Algernon had climbed in next to her. He had to coil his whole body up to fit in and his head still touched the roof. He started the engine up and a moment later the van was driving away. Harriet didn't look back. She didn't want her parents to think she was going to miss them.

The two of them didn't speak until they had reached the M4 motorway and begun the long journey east towards the city. Harriet looked for the radio, hoping to listen to music. But it had been stolen, the broken wires hanging out of the dashboard. She was aware of Algernon examining her out of the corner of his eye even as he drove and when this became too irritating she finally spoke.

"So tell me about this restaurant of yours," she said.

"What do you want to know?" Algernon asked.

"I don't know . . ."

"It's very exclusive," Algernon began. "In fact it's so exclusive that very few people know about it. Even so, it is full every night. We never advertise but word gets around. You could say that it's word of mouth. Yes. Word of mouth is very much what we're about."

There was something creepy about the way he said that. Once again his tongue slid over his lips. He smiled to himself, as if at some secret joke.

"Is it an expensive restaurant?" Harriet asked.

"Oh yes. It is the most expensive restaurant in London. Do you know how much dinner for two at my restaurant would cost you?"

Harriet shrugged.

"Five hundred pounds. And that's not including the wine."

"That's crazy!" Harriet scowled. "Nobody would pay that much for a dinner for two."

"My clients are more than happy to pay. You see . . ." Algernon smiled again. His eyes never left the road. "There are people who make lots of money in their lives. Film stars and writers. Investment bankers and businessmen. They have millions and millions of pounds and they have to spend it on something. These people think nothing of spending a hundred pounds on a few spoonfuls of caviar. They'll spend a thousand pounds on a single bottle of wine! They go to all the smartest restaurants and they don't care how much they pay as long as their meal is cooked by a famous cook, ideally with the menu written in French and all the ingredients flown, at huge expense, from all around the world. Are you with me, my dear?"

"Don't call me 'my dear'," Harriet said.

Algernon chuckled softly. "But of course there comes a time," he went on, "when they've eaten everything there is to be had. The best smoked salmon and the finest fillet steak. There are only so many ingredients in the world, my dear, and soon they find they've tasted them all. Oh yes, there are a thousand ways to prepare them. Pigeon's breast with marmalade and foie gras. Smoked sea bass with shallots and Shitaki mushrooms. But there comes a time when they feel they've had it all. When their appetites become jaded. When they're looking for a completely different eating experience. And that's when they come to Sawney Bean."

"Why did you give the restaurant such a stupid name?" Harriet asked.

"It's named after a real person," Algernon replied. He didn't seem ruffled at all even though Harriet had been purposefully trying to annoy him. "Sawney Bean lived in Scotland at the start of the century. He had unusual tastes . . ."

"I hope you're not expecting me to work in this restaurant."

"To work?" Algernon smiled. "Oh no. But I do expect you to appear in it. In fact, I'm planning to introduce you at dinner tonight . . ."

The dream shifted forward and suddenly they were in London, making their way down the King's Road, in Chelsea. And there was the restaurant! Harriet saw a small, white-bricked building with the name written in red letters above the door. The restaurant had no window and there was no menu on display. In fact, if Algernon hadn't pointed it out she wouldn't have noticed it at all. He indicated and the van turned into a narrow alley, running behind the building.

"Is this where you live?" Harriet asked. "Is this where I'm going to live?"

"For the next few hours," Algernon replied. He pulled up at the end of the alley in a small courtyard surrounded on all sides by high brick walls. There was a row of dustbins and a single door, sheet metal with several locks. "Here we go," he said.

Harriet got out of the van and as she did so the door opened and a short, fat man came out, dressed entirely in white. The man seemed to be Japanese. He had pale orange skin and slanting eyes. There

155

was a chef's hat balanced on his head. When he smiled, three gold teeth glinted in the afternoon light.

"You got her!" he exclaimed. He had a strong oriental accent.

"Yes. This is Harriet." Algernon had once again unfolded himself from the van.

"Do you know how much she weigh?" the chef asked.

"I haven't weighed her yet."

The chef ran his eyes over her. Harriet was beginning to feel more and more uneasy. The way the

man was examining her . . . well, she could almost have been a piece of meat. "She very good," he murmured.

"Young and spoilt," Algernon replied. He gestured at the door. "This way, my dear."

"What about my cases?"

"You won't need those."

Harriet was nervous now. She wasn't sure why but it was not knowing that made her feel all the worse. Perhaps it was the name. Sawney Bean. Now that she thought about it, she *did* know. She'd heard that name on a television programme or perhaps she'd read it in a book. Certainly she knew it. But how?

She allowed the two men to lead her into the restaurant and flinched as the solid metal door swung shut behind her. She found herself in a gleaming kitchen, all white-tiled surfaces, industrial-sized cookers, and gleaming pots and pans. The restaurant was closed. It was about three o'clock in the afternoon. Lunch was over. It was still some time until dinner.

She became aware that Algernon and the chef were staring at her silently, both with the same excited, hungry eyes. Sawney Bean! *Where* had she heard the name?

"She perfect," the chef said.

"That's what I thought," Algernon agreed.

"A bit fatty perhaps . . ."

"I'm not fat!" Harriet exclaimed. "Anyway, I've decided I don't like it here. I want to go home. You can take me straight back."

Algernon laughed softly. "It's too late for that," he said. "Much too late. I've paid a great deal of money for you, my dear. And I told you, we want you here for dinner tonight."

"Maybe we start by poaching her in white wine," the chef said. "Then later tonight with a Béarnaise sauce . . ."

And that was when Harriet remembered. Sawney Bean. She had read about him in a book of horror stories.

Sawney Bean.

The cannibal.

She opened her mouth to scream but no sound came out. Of course, it's impossible to scream when you're having a bad dream. You try to scream but your mouth won't obey you. Nothing will come out. That was what was happening to Harriet. She could feel the scream welling up inside her. She could see Algernon and the chef closing in on her. The room was spinning, the pots and pans dancing around her head, and still the scream wouldn't come. And then she was sucked into a vortex and the last thing she remembered was a hand reaching out to support her so she wouldn't bruise herself, wouldn't damage her flesh when she fell.

Mercifully, that was when she woke up.

It had all been a horrible dream.

Harriet opened her eyes slowly. It was the most delicious moment of her life, to know that everything that had happened *hadn't* happened. Her father hadn't gone bankrupt. Her parents hadn't sold her to some creep in a white van. Fifi would still be there to help her get dressed and serve up the breakfast. She would get up and go to school and in a few weeks' time she and her mother would leave on their Caribbean cruise. She was annoyed that such a ridiculous dream should have frightened her so much. On the other hand, it had seemed so realistic.

She lifted a hand to rub her forehead.

Or tried to.

Her hands were tied behind her. Harriet opened her eyes wide. She was lying on a marble slab in a kitchen. A huge pot of water was boiling on a stove. A Japanese chef was chopping onions with a glinting stainless steel knife.

Harriet opened her mouth.

This time she was able to scream.

School Dinners

Jamie Rix

There are some boys and girls who like school dinners. There are others who detest them.

I knew a boy once called Elgin. We used to call him Bluebottle, because he had the manners of a house fly. To say that he liked school food would not do him justice. He worshipped it. He would quite literally fall to his knees at the end of every meal and bow his head in the direction of Matron (any other school would have called her the dinner lady, but my school liked to pretend it was posh, so it *had* to be Matron). For ages I thought he was just being polite, but when I realized that he was in fact licking everyone else's dinner droppings off the floorboards under the table, it made me feel quite sick.

"You are disgusting!" I'd shout.

Elgin's head would appear over the table top, his mouth brimming with pork fat and cauliflower leaves. "Yum, yum," he'd say. "Deeelicious!"

As if this behaviour was not enough to convince me that human beings were still basically animals, who *just happened* to be able to drive cars, Elgin had one further trick up his grubby little sleeve. In the middle of each table was a slop bowl, into which every child would scrape the bits of their meal that they couldn't eat. The fat, the bones, the slugs, the grit and occasionally the potatoes. After he had hoovered up under the table, Elgin would grab the slop bowl, wave it about over his head and enquire if there were any takers. Then, while the rest of us closed our eyes and fought back the rising nausea in our throats, Elgin would down the contents of this bowl in one.

Afterwards he'd always burp, and always say, "Pardon me! Mustn't forget my manners."

I shared a table with Elgin for five years. Little wonder then that over a period of time I slowly came to loathe the sight of school dinners. You cannot imagine how I suffered when Matron slapped a dollop of stewed peas, six pieces of bacon rind and a hunk of liver, still packed full of rubber tubes, on to my plate. She might as well have given me a cowpat to eat. I think I would have preferred it.

My parents got very angry with me. They told me I was stupid and selfish. That there were hungry people who'd give their right arms to eat what I chose to throw away. I would have been happy to send it to them, but Elgin had always eaten my leftovers before I had a chance to wrap them up.

Sometimes, just to please my parents, I would try to look on the bright side.

"What's for pudding?" I'd say cheerfully, as Matron dumped the watery meat stew into my bowl.

"Lumpy, cold rice with sweet cherry jam," she'd reply, "or prunes!"

Was there no escaping this living hell?

The answer, sadly, was no.

I was plagued by Matron. She had got wind of the

fact that I did not like my school food and used to shadow me around the dining hall. She lurked behind stacks of freezing cold hot-plates, she loitered by the serving hatch, and worst, and most embarrassing of all, she would follow me into the toilet to check that I was not spitting my food out.

"If you don't eat the food, young man," she said to me one day, as I sat staring at a plate of kedgeree, "you will sit here till it gets cold."

"But it's cold already!" I said. "That's why I can't eat it."

Her nostrils flared. "Then you will sit here until it gets even colder or until it's full of maggots, whichever is the sooner!"

"But it's full of maggots already!" I said. "That's why I can't eat it."

Her eye started to twitch. "Then you will sit here until *you* are full of maggots," she said triumphantly.

I didn't want to die in the school dining-room.

"Now eat it!" she screamed. A little drop of saliva dripped from the corner of her mouth and settled, like a money spider, on my food. Then she stood over me until I had eaten every last morsel.

This sort of thing went on most days. I got into such a panic about what Matron was going to force me to eat for lunch, that I asked my parents to write me a note, saying that I was the only person in the world suffering from a rare disease called Schooldinnerphobia. This was a most unfortunate affliction which meant that if I ate school dinners I would die, instantly, and the person who was in charge of my table would immediately be sent to prison for the rest of her life, for murder. Matron always looked after our table, so I thought that she would probably get the message.

Much to my surprise, my parents sent a note to Matron, along these lines, and it seemed to have the right effect. The day I brought the note in, I was excused from eating school dinner. Matron made me eat the note instead!

I'm sure that had it not been for my unfortunate association with Elgin and Matron I would have had much the same attitude as any other child towards school dinners. As it was, though, I was seriously disturbed. I could not sleep for dreaming of huge, rancid chops leaping out from behind doors, pressing me to the ground and demanding to be eaten. The smell of boiled cabbage and burned custard returned to me with increasing frequency, and then one day, when I was twenty-two years old, I had my first flashback.

I was standing in a tightly packed lift, minding my own business and watching out for my floor, when suddenly my stomach started churning. As I tried to pretend to the onlookers in the lift that it was not *my* stomach making that awful grumbling noise, my mouth joined in. My jaws started to chomp of their own accord. My throat started salivating and the revolting stench of greasy spotted dick filled my nostrils. People were staring at me. I was chewing my tongue like a madman. I tried to smile, but whenever I did I just burped, and every time I burped, a lump of spotted dick popped, from nowhere, into my mouth. I couldn't spit it out, not in front of all those people, so, to my complete disgust, I was forced to eat it . . . just as I had been forced to eat spotted dick by Matron, all those years before.

My school dinners had come back to haunt me.

From this day on, things went from bad to worse. The very sight or smell of food would trigger the most alarming responses from within my body. If someone was cooking baked beans I found myself crawling under their kitchen table and shouting: "No! No! NO! I won't come out. I HATE baked beans!"

Carrots had a similar effect *and* tomato ketchup, especially if it reeked of vinegar. I had lost control. Something had taken me over, and I was completely at its mercy.

One night, I took my girlfriend to a very posh restaurant. It was an important evening for me and I was desperate to leave her with the impression that I was a cool, laid-back guy, whom it was well worth getting to know better. The waiter took our coats and showed us to a candlelit table for two in the corner.

"Perfect," I thought, "she's going to love this."

The menu was superb. Lobster, medallions of beef, grilled sole, lamb noisettes and countless other dishes that could not have reminded me *less* of those poisonous school dinners. It was a great relief. I felt confident, for the first time in months, that I was not going to experience a psychic flashback. At the bottom of the menu there was a special notice printed in gold ink. It read:

FOR THE PERFECT NIGHT OUT, WHY
NOT TRY OUR CHEF'S SPECIALITY
ONLY £125 FOR 2 persons

How could I resist? I ordered champagne, the chef's speciality for two, and sat back to gaze deeply into my loved one's eyes.

A few minutes later, three trumpeters approached our table, stood to attention behind my chair and blew a fanfare. The other people in the restaurant stopped eating and turned to look. The Head Waiter emerged from the kitchens wheeling a trolley, with a huge gold plate on it. The restaurant applauded, my girlfriend laughed, and the Chef's Speciality was ceremoniously brought to our table.

What an evening this was turning out to be.

"With the compliments of the chef," said the Head Waiter, taking the lid off the gold plate.

My stomach lurched, my throat tightened and I could hear Matron chiding me to eat it all up, or else.

"No, I won't!" I shouted, pulling the tablecloth off the table and upsetting champagne all over my girlfriend. "You can't make me!"

"Monsieur," said the Head Waiter, who was a little alarmed. "Is it not to your liking?"

"I HATE FISH CAKES!" I wailed. "THEY MAKE ME THROW UP!"

Everyone was watching me now, but I wasn't aware of them. I was back in school. Even the Head Waiter had started to look like Matron.

"Eat it up, Monsieur," he said.

"Won't! Won't! Won't! Won't!" I said clamping my lips tightly shut.

"I shall tell your mummy how naughty you have been!" said the waiter.

"Don't care! Can't eat fish cakes!" I yelled. Then I threw a bread roll at him, and disappeared under the table.

My girlfriend had started crying by now. In fact she'd left. She had never been so embarrassed in all her life. I could see her point.

The Head Waiter was trying Matron's old trick.

"Shall we park Daddy's car in the garage?" he said holding out a spoonful of fish cake. Then he added, "Brmmm Brmmm! See what a shiny red car it is!"

I poked my head above the table to look, and he grabbed my chin, forcing my mouth open.

"Open the garage doors!" he said loudly. "Because here it comes!"

I yelled and kicked and thumped the table as he tried to force the food into my mouth. I even spat some in his face. In the end, though, I must have eaten the fish cake, because when I woke up on the pavement outside the restaurant it was all round my mouth, like a breadcrumb moustache.

This all happened many years ago. I'm an old man now. Most of my life has been spent in the shadow of this terrible haunting. I still have flashbacks if I see an advert for mashed potato or pass a café selling black chips, but I have found that by living alone and seeing no one, I have been able to keep the ghost of school dinners more or less at bay.

Unfortunately next week is my eighty-third birthday, and I am going to live in an Old People's Home. I won't pretend I'm happy about it, because I'm not. You see, there's a Matron there (a very familiar-looking Matron), who has promised me that the first thing she's going to do when I arrive is start feeding me up!

Of Polymuf Stock

John Christopher

I was born true man, but of polymuf stock.

Until I was nine I knew nothing of this. I was the son of Andrew Harding, chief of the Captains. I had an elder brother and two elder sisters, and lived in the Harding house which looked proudly at the palace from across the square. I had a nurse and servants to do my bidding.

One day, having quarrelled with a friend, I found myself alone in a part of the city, near the East Gate, I had rarely visited. The streets were mean, the houses pinched and crowded, and there were smells that made me wrinkle my nose. A dead cat in the gutter must have been there a week.

In one rotting street three boys followed me. Their tunics were of cheap cloth and both their clothes and they would have been better for washing. They jeered at me; then came past and planted themselves in my path. One demanded my name and I told him:

Harding. It proved they were Blainites.

The Hardings and the Blaines had been rivals for generations. This was normally concealed under a show of politeness but at a lower level, among their followers, the feud was open. The three young Blainites were delighted to find a solitary Harding in their territory. They would not have dared touch me, since I was noble, but taunts leave no traces. In the end it was I who turned violent, launching myself at my chief tormentor, who happened to be the biggest.

Had things been equal I would have been no match for him, because he was used to rough fighting. But he was held back by awareness of my rank, and probably by the thought of retribution. I had no such scruples and was rubbing his face in the dirt when we were pulled apart and lifted to our feet. A crowd had collected.

Questions were asked, my name required again. One man asked:

"Isak! The one who . . ."

His voice dropped to a whisper I could not catch. I heard other whispers and saw glances exchanged. It meant nothing at the time except that they were Blainites. I noticed with satisfaction that my recent opponent was crying, and turned away. I had gone several paces when a voice called:

"Polymuf! The Harding polymuf brat."

That meant nothing either, being plain nonsense. I knew I bore no malformation of the body. I walked on, towards the city centre. Boys followed, chanting:

"Polymuf . . . polymuf!"

It was some stupidity the Blainites had devised to insult their betters. I came into Bird Street where troopers were comparing notes on caged finches, and the boys fell back and left me.

A few days later, I heard the jeer repeated in the street. I still did not think it mattered or I would not have spoken casually of it to David Greene. He knew nothing either, but he asked, and was told, and told me.

Every child born had to be taken to the Seer, to be scrutinized for defects of the body. Those with none were classed as true men, the short-legged ones as dwarfs. The rest, even where the defect was no more than a missing finger, were polymufs, who must serve true men, who had no rights and could hold no property.

A rejected child of human stock was given to a dwarf or polymuf foster-mother for rearing. The reverse was also true. And this, David said, had been my case. I had been brought to the Seance Hall by polymuf parents, judged true man by the

Seer, and given to the Hardings.

I listened in disbelieving horror. David's eyes watched me. He was not smiling but I read the smile behind them, and more: pity, contempt. I said:

"That's a lie!"

He shrugged. "Perhaps. It is what they say."

I made an excuse to leave him, and ran home. It was a cold grey morning, threatening rain. The doorman rose from his stool to salute me, heaving up his twisted body.

My nurse Betty was in my room. The housemaids had cleaned it, but she must always do a final setting to rights. As long as I could remember I had taken questions to her for answering, troubles for soothing. But when she looked at me from her single eye, I could not speak. From infancy the deformity had meant nothing, but now I turned and ran. She called but I paid no heed.

I ran across the courtyard, heading for the stables. As I reached them, I collided with someone coming out. I was checked and held. My father's voice said:

"What haste, boy?" I looked up, but could not speak. "And tears? A Harding does not cry, when he is nine years old."

I said, gasping: "A Harding, sir? Or a polymuf's brat?"

He stared at me, his face closed and seeming hard.

I thought he might strike me, and almost welcomed it. But he said:

"We have talking to do, Isak. Come."

He was not a tall man, and sparely built. His face too was thin, with keen blue eyes and a well trimmed beard, turning white. It had never occurred to me to look for a resemblance to my own heavy features in his. I did so now, then turned my head away.

We sat in his business room, with the parchment rent rolls hanging on sticks on the wall and logs crackling noisily in the hearth. He was a man who felt the cold and sought warmth where he could. He sat in his chair, covered with the chestnut hide of a favourite horse that had been killed under him in battle, I on a leather stool before him.

"The tears have stopped," he said. "Good. Now, tell me what you have heard."

I would have broken down in the telling except that his unblinking eyes forbade it. When I had finished, I asked:

"Is it true, sir?"

He nodded. "As far as it goes."

I began to sob, and he put a hand on my shoulder.

"A Harding does not cry."

"But I am none!"

"You are."

"I am not your son."

174

"No," he said. "But of my line and blood. You are my grandson, Isak."

I stared, uncomprehending. He said:

"My first-born child was a girl. The Seer named her polymuf and she was taken from us. It is the law, and the Spirits command it. My wife grieved deeply and died within two winters. Later I married again and my children were whole and human. These you have called your sisters and your brother."

He paused, and I waited. "Years later the Seer came to me. A polymuf woman had borne a boy who was true man and must be given to true men for rearing. The woman was my daughter. My wife and I took you. You are my own, a Harding."

"My mother . . ."

"Has doubtless had other children."

"Who is she? Where does she live?"

He shook his head. "We do not know."

"But . . ."

"It is the law, Isak. The Seer knows, but no other may. I was not informed as to whom she was given, nor she that you were given back to me. The Seer told me of your ancestry because it seemed fitting to him. And I . . ." He paused again. "I thanked him, and the Spirits, and made an offering which he called generous. It was a poor return for what I had been given."

"And my true father?"

"Who knows?"

Who knew, indeed? I thought of polymuf men I had passed unthinkingly, with all the diversity of ugliness the evil Spirits might wreak on an unborn child. I thought of Grog, who used four arms in sweeping the street, and Petey, who had a double row of teeth which he displayed for the troopers who bought him ale. Any one might have been my father.

"And it does not matter," my grandfather said. I stared at him, hot-eyed. "You are a Harding. Those who have dared mock you will regret it."

I never knew what word went out, but there were no more cries of "Polymuf". The Hardings, as I have said, were powerful. My grandfather, having bidden me forget what I had learned, made sure none reminded me of it. But there was no need of reminder. The truth sank deep and lay with the cold weight of iron. Polymufs became monstrous to me, even Betty. I flinched from her touch and the gaze of her single eye.

It was customary for a boy of noble family to leave home at eleven for a spell in the barracks. I begged to go when I was ten, and this was granted. When I returned it was with high praise from the Drill Sergeant. I showed great promise: he had rarely known a boy so eager to excel.

The fact was that I loved the barracks, a place where no polymuf was permitted entry. I grew drunk with the smell of horses and leather, the clash of swords and the jingle of harness irons. The hardships of the life exalted me. They were trials for true men.

I made no friends and wanted none. The other boys talked, I guessed, behind my back – maybe called me polymuf when I was out of hearing. But they watched their words in my company. I did not mind if they liked or disliked me. It was enough that they dropped their eyes before mine.

The later years of my childhood passed during a time in which great events took place. Prince Stephen was deposed, and replaced by Robert Perry. Intrigue and murder followed and within two years Robert's son Peter was Prince, and his younger son taken to live with the High Seers in Sanctuary. Subsequently Luke returned, and fought and killed his brother, and became Prince, our third within three years. And the following spring, being thirteen, I was named to fight in the Contest.

In this yearly tournament, four sons of Captains led teams of four, which were eliminated in turn as their Captains were unhorsed. The swords were wooden, but they could hurt. It was no sport for weaklings.

My first requirement was to find the best men for my team. My reputation helped. I was known as the best swordsman and one of the two best horsemen of my year; and the followers of the winning Captain would receive gold. To those I canvassed I promised a double sum, relying on my grandfather's pride to make good the promise. Then I drilled them, relentlessly.

Finally I made alliances. It often happened that two Young Captains would agree to fight together first, to eliminate a third. Robin Becket, my chief rival, offered such an arrangement. I accepted, but found excuse not to seal it with a handshake. Then I went to Peter Gray, whose team was reckoned third in strength, and made a bargain for the first round, and this time sealed it.

Robin was confused and shaken when Peter and I rode against him, and put up little opposition. It took less than five minutes' fighting to bring his fall, and the first interval. When the fight resumed I set my men at Peter and here again had the advantage of surprise: our agreement had been for the first round but he had assumed we would keep our alliance to eliminate the fourth Captain, Ranald. Ranald gladly joined us in attacking Peter: to survive into the final round was more honour than he could have hoped for.

Peter fought hard, and three of Ranald's men went down before my sword got him under the ribs and dropped him from his saddle. We waited calmly for the third bell, drove Ranald quickly into a corner, and overthrew him.

It was the shortest Contest in memory, the first for many years in which a team had won without losing a man. As I led my pony to the Prince's pavilion, cheers echoed against the bright sky and bushy top of Catherine's Hill. No one shouted "Polymuf". Prince Luke, only a few years older than myself, proffered the hilt of the jewelled sword, which was the victor's prize. He said:

"You fight well, Isak."

"Thank you, sire."

"But hard. The surgeon says Peter has a broken rib from that last thrust of yours."

"Must one not fight hard in battle, sire?"

"In battle, yes."

He looked as though he might say more, but did not. I lifted the sword to salute him, and the crowd howled louder still.

My victory was not popular among my peers. It was whispered that Robin, feeling cheated, would challenge me to a duel. When I heard that, I sought him out where he sat with friends on the steps of the Buttercross. I stood and looked at him, and he looked away.

I had grown accustomed to my own company and it contented me. Sometimes at night I stood on the city wall, looking down the Itchen valley, and thought of the future. It was through arms that a man achieved glory, but wealth set the seal on success. My grandfather had been a notable warrior, but he owed his position in the city to the prosperity of his farms. Soldiering was not an end but a means. In war one stood to gain booty, and the better one fought the more one got. I vowed I would earn a lion's share. Gregory was my father's elder son and heir, but the day would come when my riches outranked his.

Wealth signified power also. Men had believed no commoner could rise to be Prince, but the Perrys had given the lie to that. They would say it was unthinkable that someone born of polymuf stock could reign. But it was not unthinkable, for I thought it.

I toughened body and mind for the task I had set myself. In the city streets I walked alone and others gave me room. I scarcely saw them. The ones I did notice were the polymufs. That one, the spindly giant nearly eight feet tall: was he my father? And the stooping woman, with a cloth pulled across to hide her face: was she my mother?

On my first campaign I was a scout only, but it made a start. We rode against Romsey, whose army marshalled on the far bank of the river on which the city stood; then edged south along the valley, our army shadowing them across the water. Two days passed in this fashion. It was something that the weather held fair: cloudy, but warm and dry.

On the second night I was given a post on the southern flank, on high ground from which, at dawn, I might spy the Romsey outriders. As evening faded into night the sky emptied of cloud and the air grew calm. White mist rose from the river and spread out.

It reached me in the small hours, a chill miasma

that stung throat and eyes. That was a long watch. The mist stifled the small sounds of the night – the owl's cry, the swish of grass or crackle of thicket at an animal's passing. At last, very slowly, the blackness turned to grey, the grey to pearl. But no more than that. I could distinguish a brightness in the east, but the fingers on my outstretched hand were shadowy. I could scarcely see my feet.

I could do no good here, and the mist might last all day, so I decided to rejoin the army. I could not see my way, though, and a scout does not call for help. It was, I thought, a simple matter of heading downhill till I reached the river, then turning right. But the slope did not run continually downwards. There was an intervening ridge and there, unable to see beyond a foot or two ahead, I must have turned south instead of west.

Eventually I knew I was lost. But the mist seemed to be thinning: the brighter pearl of the east was tinged with fitful yellow and at last with gold. A pale disc came and went. Then clear sun, and mist lifting all round.

I was surrounded by rabbit-cropped grass patched with scrub. I could see nothing of the river, but a thorned mound offered a vantage point. Loose bricks underfoot told me this was a ruin from days before the Disaster. Simple people thought such places the haunts of evil Spirits, bound there by the perdition into which they had led mankind, and shunned them. That did not trouble me. Even when the slope collapsed beneath my feet and I found myself falling, I did not think of Spirits – merely cursed my foolishness in not taking more care.

I landed painfully but broke no bones. A jagged hole, high up, gave little light. I felt in my pack for tinder-box and candle.

I had crashed into a room which, apart from the rubble that had fallen with me, was untouched. I saw a table and a sideboard, holding objects covered with dust. As I went near, wax from my candle melted and dropped, burning a hole in spider webs and revealing a yellow gleam beneath.

I looked more closely. Pots and plates, salvers, jugs, vases . . . some gold, the rest, though tarnished, plainly silver. I discovered a wide silver dish worked in delicate patterns, and a heavy chain of gold. There were cupboards beneath the sideboard, holding more treasure: a large silver bowl was heaped with smaller ones.

Here was greater booty than a warrior might hope to gain in a score of campaigns, undisturbed for more than a hundred years. It had no owner but the Spirits, and they could have little use for it. I was rich – richer maybe than my grandfather Harding.

Caution succeeded excitement. Even if I could carry all this away, it would be unwise to try. I must take no more than a pot or two. But I could mark the place, and come back whenever I wished and get what I needed. This was barren land, close to one of the great ruins. No one would willingly venture near.

I took a small gold pot and plate, and put them in my pack. When I was older . . . Gold would buy not only houses, farms, servants, but also men. I would have more followers than the Blaines and Hardings put together. And buying men bought power; power enough to take the city, and other cities.

There was a door beyond the table which opened easily. On the far side were buckets, made of that substance called plast, which countrymen, when they turn it up in digging, are careful to burn, washing their hands afterwards. A blue bucket and two yellow ones were heaped with bracelets, brooches and other jewellery of gold set with precious stones. This was not just riches, but wealth incalculable.

I looked further, and saw more: a wooden chest, laden with jewels, a long string of pearls spilling over the edge . . . and a bed, where a figure lay.

He was dead, but I felt no fear of that either. I expected to see the gleam of bone, but flesh still covered him – dried dark, drawn tight from grinning teeth and blackened eyeholes, but preserved. He had died in a dry summer, perhaps, and his flesh had withered instead of rotting. It sometimes happens.

Any such relic of a face would look mean and pinched, but I wondered if his features had in fact changed so much. It was he who had brought the treasure to this spot. When the Disaster struck, and great cities tumbled like play bricks, survivors had fled into the country for safety. But he had gone back into the ruins, risking earthquake and plague, to dig for gold. They had been a rich people, our ancestors, and there had been much to find. He had carried it here, load upon load. A dozen trinkets lay on the bed beside him, like the toys a child puts by its pillow. On his bony wrist were three small clocks, secured by gold bracelets.

How long had he lived here? For years, certainly – such a hoard could not have been amassed in less time. And how died? Of sickness, or old age? Or perhaps of hunger, with no food in reach and unwilling to leave his treasure to search for it.

In the Disaster the world had been shattered into ugly fragments, people had died in numbers none could imagine; and he had huddled here, counting his wealth by candlelight. He had withered away until death came, then withered further. He had altered scarcely more than his changeless gold. Even the rats had shunned him.

Now at last fear came to me, though it had nothing to do either with corpse or Spirits. It was rather a misery that struck deep, a feeling of hopelessness biting into heart and bones. I had a desperate need to leave this place, not because of its ghosts but because it held none – nothing but emptiness and desolation, and barren treasure.

I went back to the other room. The hole in the ceiling was out of reach, but with the table upended . . . I dragged it from the wall, sending its cobwebbed cargo clattering to the ground, and scrambled on top. Would the broken laths take my weight? I leaped, felt the edge give, but clawed my way up to reach a beam. Straddling it, with the way open to the sky and the world outside, I felt in my pack for the golden pot and plate, pitched them down and heard them crash in the darkness.

The day was bright, with no more than a white steam coming up from the ground, the sky clear except for wispy cloud. I found the river, and followed it north. Ten minutes later I reached a village, and hurried towards it, joyful at the sound of a dog's bark, the sight of smoking chimneys. At the outskirts a man drew water from a well. He wore servant's clothes, and as he turned I saw one eye had a cast and his right arm was crooked.

He bowed his head. "Greetings, master."

I looked at him, and did not shrink away.

I said: "Greetings, brother."

Best Before

Laurie Channer

Mackenzie pushed the leftovers and the limp celery aside to see all the way into the back of the refrigerator. The plastic yogurt tub was still there. Her dad hadn't seen it yet, or he would have thrown it out ages ago. It was blue-and-white and looked perfectly normal. But Mackenzie was afraid to open it. It had been there a long time. It would be really nasty inside. Green and fuzzy with mould, or maybe even *blue* and fuzzy. Mackenzie had even seen bright *purple* mould once. And the longer it stayed, the worse it would get.

She crouched there, looking way into the bottom shelf. The kitchen rubbish was right nearby. She could just grab the container quickly and throw it straight in the bin without opening it.

Mackenzie reached in.

And it moved.

She yelped and yanked her arm back. The lid was

bulging up. And up. But it stayed tight. So tight, it looked like it could pop off with just a little touch.

Mackenzie thought about the horrible, stinky air that was building up inside the yogurt tub. She couldn't get rid of it without the smell making the whole house reek. Her dad would be mad for sure. Especially if the smell didn't go away for days, like skunk.

She put the other things back inside, making sure they hid, but didn't touch, the container. She shut the fridge door quickly and then froze, wondering if she'd slammed it hard enough to shake it into bursting. For a moment she stood, waiting to hear the "pop". It didn't come. Not yet.

Mackenzie ran out of the kitchen.

"Did you open it?" Jason asked. He was on his bike in her driveway.

Mackenzie sat down to put on her roller blades. "No way," she shook her head. "*I'm* not opening it." It was on a dare from Jason, her best friend, that she'd first pushed the yogurt tub to the back of the fridge. That was way before school let out for summer vacation. They were each going to let something go bad in their fridges. The winner would be the one who could make Roddy Blandings throw up. "The top goes like this now," she said, and traced the rounded shape in the air.

"Cool!" Jason said. "You're so lucky that you don't have a mum. My cheese was just getting really fuzzy when she found it and threw it away."

"My dad never cleans the fridge," Mackenzie said. But she was worried. Jason's mum had thrown his thing out, almost right after they'd started. Mackenzie had just forgotten about hers until yesterday, when Roddy had thrown up from being on the swings at the park. That reminded her. Now it was a week before school started again and the container had been in there all that time. By now it might make *her* throw up.

"Eeeew!" Jason said. "What if it goes off like a stink bomb? Blammo! Yucky stuff all over your kitchen. Then the Experts will have to come!"

Mackenzie didn't want that. They'd all heard about the Consumables Disposal Experts who had to be called when something went really bad in somebody's house, but none of the kids in the neighbourhood had ever seen them. The Experts were scary men in big, black rubbery coats with a mysterious truck that they dumped the bad stuff into. Roddy said that they put whoever was responsible for the stuff going bad into the truck as well, in a gunk tank with all the yuck they collected.

"They wouldn't come just for a yogurt container,"

Mackenzie said. She hoped it was true.

"You better throw it away now," Jason said.

"No way!" Mackenzie cried. "It might go blammo! when I touch it!"

"Then you better tell your dad," Jason said.

"He's at work," Mackenzie said. "I can't call him unless it's an emergency." Her dad was a landscaper and was at a different place every day.

"It *will* be an emergency when that thing goes blammo!" Jason laughed. "I'm getting out of here!" He hopped up on the pedals and started riding his bike towards the park.

Mackenzie looked anxiously back at the house, then tore off after him on her skates, yelling, "Wait up!" the whole way.

It was lunchtime when they wheeled back to their street. Right away they knew something was wrong. They stopped at the corner and stared.

"Hey, that's your house," Jason said, like Mackenzie couldn't see it for herself.

A big, black truck was parked right in front of Mackenzie's house. It was much bigger than Mackenzie's dad's pickup that usually sat there. Wide, yellow tape went all the way from the truck, up the front walk of her house and right in the door, which was open. The truck had a huge, concrete, canister-shaped thing on wheels towed along behind it. The thing had a lid like a sewer cover with a giant hinge.

"It's them!" Jason said. "And there's the gunk tank!"

Mackenzie got a very bad feeling in her stomach. The Consumables Disposal Experts were in her house. That thing in the fridge must have gone *blammo*! after all. And her dad wasn't even home from work yet. "Let's go back to the park," she said. But she couldn't move.

Neighbours were standing on their lawns watching. The grown-ups were hanging on to their kids, not letting them go near the truck. There were rumours that just the smell coming out of the gunk tank would kill someone if they got too close. Mackenzie wondered if the smell from the yogurt tub would do the same thing. She sniffed the air a little bit, but didn't smell anything.

Two large men in big, black, buckled coats, big, buckled boots and shiny helmets came out of the front door of her house. They looked around, and their faces were hidden by scary bug-eyed gas masks. They wore air tanks like back-packs, and gloves, thick, rubbery ones that reached way up towards their elbows, swallowing the sleeves of their coats. All up and down the street, people took a step back when they came down the walk. Tiffany Wilkes ran

from her mother and straight into her own house, banging the screen door as she ran inside.

The men took some equipment – heavy, long-handled tongs, and a big plastic bin and some other stuff – from the truck and carried it back inside.

Jason rode over to the nearest grown-up. The woman was standing in her driveway, pretending to wash her car, but watching just like everybody else. "Excuse me, ma'am," he said. "What's going on? That's her house," he pointed to Mackenzie, who wanted to hide.

The lady frowned at Mackenzie. "There must be

something in there that's a risk to the neighbourhood. It's very serious when the Experts have to come out. They're going to do an extraction."

"But we didn't call them!" Mackenzie said. "We aren't even home!" She wondered how they knew what she'd done.

"Oh, they can go right in if they need to," the lady said. "They're like the police that way." She gave Mackenzie a stern look. "And if nobody called them, it must be *very* serious indeed. You go over and tell them you live there. They'll want to see you."

Mackenzie didn't know that one little container could be a danger to the whole street. She also didn't like the sound of the word "extraction". It sounded like what they'd do to a ten-year-old who'd caused trouble. Extract her and put her in the gunk tank.

Mackenzie skated away as fast as she could.

She went back to the park. It was empty. Every other kid was back on her street, watching the Experts.

Mackenzie swung on the swings, but it wasn't any fun. She stared at the ground and wondered if she could ever go home.

"Mackenzie!"

She looked up to see a man arriving at the park. A big man in a big, black coat and boots and helmet. He was coming straight for her, calling her name.

They knew! Mackenzie jumped off the swings to run away. But she forgot she was still in her roller blades and fell down hard in the grass. The man was running towards her now, in his black, scary, flapping rubber, like a bat, or a giant kid-eating bird. Mackenzie tried to run in her skates, but the grass was all bumpy and she stumbled again, twisting her ankle. She couldn't get up. The Expert's boots thumped closer behind her. She screamed and shut her eyes tight as he swooped down and grabbed her.

"Don't run, Mackenzie!"

Mackenzie howled and kicked. He scooped her up. "You have to come back with me," he said in a firm, deep voice.

She was going in the gunk tank, she knew it. "No! No!" she cried. She struggled as hard as she could. "Don't take me away!"

Mackenzie suddenly felt herself put down on the grass. The Expert squatted down and peered right into her face. "Mackenzie, just what do you think we're doing here?"

He wasn't wearing the bug mask any more, but under the helmet, he was scowling. Mackenzie was still frightened. "You took some stuff out of my fridge and now you're going to put me in the gunk tank," she said, the tears starting.

"We have a job to do to protect people," the Expert

said. "There are a lot of nasty things around, nastier than they used to be. Things that cause sickness and disease. We can't let a germ get out and make your whole neighbourhood sick. Now we need the number to reach your dad."

"My dad won't let you put me in the gunk tank!"

The Expert sat back and took off his fireman-type helmet. "Who told you that? You're not going in the tank!"

"Oh." For the first time, Mackenzie noticed that he had wavy brown hair, the same colour as her dad's. "I'm not?"

The Expert reached out his big hand. Mackenzie ducked, but he just ruffled her hair. "Not if you help us do our jobs," he said and his eyes crinkled when he smiled.

Mackenzie stood on the porch of her house, while the Experts put their stuff away and rolled up the yellow tape. They were finished in her house now and they both had their black gear off. Underneath the coats they wore blue uniform shirts and trousers that looked like the green ones Mackenzie's dad wore to work. They left the boots on. The second Expert had blond hair.

The neighbourhood kids, including Jason, watched the Experts and then Mackenzie, like she was important now too.

The Expert with the crinkly eyes went into the truck and came back out with something. It was a yogurt container with the brand name *Metro* in red on it. "Here," he said. "We cleaned it out. You can have it. The kid always gets to keep the container."

Mackenzie suddenly felt a very bad feeling. This wasn't her container. This other tub, it had been a new one her dad bought just last week. It had been in the front of the fridge. *Her* stuff was in a *blue*-and-white tub. A bulging blue-and-white tub. Maybe they hadn't seen it at the back of the bottom shelf. And hers didn't have just yogurt in it. She'd put bits of a whole bunch of different things that could go bad in. She'd even put in fertilizer from her dad's truck. She never told Jason that part, in case he thought it was cheating.

Mackenzie wanted to tell the men, but she couldn't. They might not be friendly any more if they knew she was growing something bad on purpose. But she also felt funny about not telling.

She could hear the blond one in the living-room, phoning to her dad. "The checkout scanner at the Food Mart told us everyone who bought a certain kind of yogurt," he said. "Metro brand, 250 milli-litres, plain, set style. It's a very, very bad batch. Contaminated at the dairy. Good thing no one had eaten any of it yet. I'm sorry, sir that we don't have time to give you the courtesy cleaning of the whole fridge, but we have a lot of stops to make. You might think about throwing that celery away, though."

Mackenzie slipped past him into the kitchen and stood in front of the fridge. It didn't look any different from before. But there was still something bad inside.

Through the open front door, she could hear doors slamming shut on the truck. Another few seconds and it would be too late to tell the Experts. Mackenzie still wasn't sure. Maybe if she looked again . . .

As she reached for the fridge handle, she heard a sudden, loud "pop". Mackenzie stopped with her hand still in midair.

The fridge began to shake.

Mackenzie screamed as the door flew open. A rotten-egg, sour-milk, rubbishey smell rushed out. She screamed again as something large and slimy and turquoisey-green grew bigger on the bottom shelf. It pushed everything out in front of it. Jars of mustard and relish smashed on to the floor. It grew taller too, changing shape all the way, knocking out the shelves above it. Milk and pop bottles burst as they hit the tiles. Stuff spattered everywhere and the thing in the fridge was still growing.

Mackenzie could only stand there, frozen to the spot. The horrible smell made her feel faint.

She didn't hear them coming, but suddenly the Experts were at the kitchen doorway. But then, the thing in the fridge leaped out at her.

It knocked her on to her back and plastered its hideous green self all over her. It was nearly as big as Mackenzie now, with vine-like limbs that it tried to wrap around her as she struggled. It was smothering her with its terrible, awful stink. She could hear the men shouting to each other.

"I'll pull it off, you get the tongs!"

She felt one of the Experts jump in to wrestle the creature away from her. It slid off and she squirmed away across the floor. It was plastered now across the Expert, the brown-haired one. She couldn't see his face under the writhing, smelly thing, just his hair. Mackenzie grabbed a bottle of disinfectant spray from the cupboard under the sink and started squirting. The creature flinched from the spray, but stayed on the man. His muffled yells were getting weaker.

The blond-haired Expert ran back into the kitchen with the heavy black tongs and swung them on to the green thing so hard Mackenzie worried about his partner underneath. Thin, white yogurt-blood spewed out in all directions. He smashed again and again. Mackenzie hid her face.

The yogurt-thing gave a hiss which became a gurgle. Suddenly everything was very quiet again.

Mackenzie opened her eyes. There was drippy yogurt goo all over the room, and the horrible green shapeless thing still wound around the Expert on the floor. "He's not moving," she said.

The blond Expert pried the creature off his partner. The man with the wavy brown hair lay very still.

"You hit him with the tongs!" Mackenzie cried.

"No," his partner said. "He suffocated under that *thing*." He knelt down. "I've never seen anything like it before." He shook his head in disbelief. "We handle food and germs, not *monsters*."

Mackenzie started to cry, right there on the floor. It was all her fault. "I'm sorry."

The Expert shook his head and looked very sad too. "No, it's our fault. We should have checked the whole fridge when we still had our masks on. That would have saved him."

He sat on the floor and put an arm round Mackenzie and stared at his partner. "He'd be glad he saved *you*," he said.

Mackenzie couldn't stop crying.

It took a long time for things to be sorted out. Mackenzie's dad got home at about the same time as the official people arrived to help the Expert put the yogurt creature in the gunk tank. The neighbourhood watched, and Roddy Blandings threw up at the sight and smell of it. Then they took the dead Expert away.

A special crew cleaned up the fridge and the goo in the kitchen. When they were done, they offered her the blue-and-white yogurt tub, all scrubbed clean. Mackenzie didn't take it.

ACKNOWLEDGEMENTS

The editor and publishers wish to thank the following for permission to use copyright material:

Ray Bradbury: for "The Veldt" from *The Stories of Ray Bradbury*, first published by Grafton Books. Copyright © 1950, renewed 1977 by Ray Bradbury, reproduced by permission of HarperCollins Publishers Ltd.

Laurie Channer: for "Best Before" from *Truly Scary Stories for Fearless Kids*, ed. Greg Ioannon, first published by Key Porter Books Ltd (1998) Copyright © 1998 Laurie Channer, reprinted by permission of the author.

John Christopher: for "Of Polymuf Stock" from *Young Winter's Tales, No. 2*, first published by Macmillan (1971). Copyright © 1971 John Christopher, reproduced by permission of the author.

Roald Dahl: for "The Surgeon" from *The Collected Short Stories of Roald Dahl*, first published by Michael Joseph Ltd (1991). Copyright © 1986 Roald Dahl, reproduced by permission of David Higham Associates on behalf of the Estate of the author.

Anthony Horowitz: for "Harriet's Horrible Dream" from *Horowitz Horror*, first published by Orchard Books (1999). Copyright © 1999 Anthony Horowitz, reproduced by permission of Orchard Books, a division of The Watts Publishing Group Ltd.

Kenneth Ireland: for "The Werewolf Mask", first published by Hodder & Stoughton (1983). Copyright © 1983 Kenneth Ireland, reproduced by permission of Jennifer Luithlen Agency on behalf of the author.

Paul Jennings: for "Spaghetti Pig-Out" from *Uncanny!* by Paul Jennings, first published by Penguin Books Australia (1988). Copyright © 1988 Paul Jennings, reproduced by permission of Penguin Books Australia Ltd.

Rob Marsh: for "The Changing" from *Tales of Mystery and Suspense* by Rob Marsh, first published by Struik Publishers (Pty) Ltd (1994). Copyright © 1994 Rob Marsh, reproduced by permission of Struik Publishers (Pty) Ltd.

Jamie Rix: for "School Dinners" from *Ghostly Tales for Ghastly Kids* by Jamie Rix, first published by Scholastic Publications Ltd (1992). Copyright © 1992 Jamie Rix, by permission of Scholastic Ltd.

Robert Swindells: for "What's for Dinner?' from *No More School?*, first published by Methuen's Children's Books (1991). Copyright © 1983 Robert Swindells, reproduced by permission of Jennifer Luithlen Agency on behalf of the author.

Every effort has been made to trace the copyright holders but where this has not been possible or where any error has been made the publishers will be pleased to make the necessary arrangement at the first opportunity.